FIERCE RESISTANCE

LAWRENCE F. BLOOM

Published by Red Penguin Books

Bellerose Village, New York

Library of Congress Control Number: 2020913942

ISBN

Print 978-1-63777-347-5

Digital 978-1-63777-348-2

This is a work of fiction.

Any resemblance to actual events, locales, or persons, living or dead, is entirely coincidental.

*I dedicate this novel, "Fierce Resistance" to the memory of my
parents,
Ruth and Jack Bloom
Forever in my heart*

L.F.B.

Contents

Foreword   vii

Chapter 1   1
Chapter 2   15
Chapter 3   35
Chapter 4   53
Chapter 5   61
Chapter 6   71
Chapter 7   79
Chapter 8   85
Chapter 9   95
Chapter 10   111
Chapter 11   119
Chapter 12   133
Chapter 13   141
Chapter 14   159
Chapter 15   165
Chapter 16   185
Chapter 17   191

Acknowledgments   195
About the Author   197

Foreword

In the 1930s and 1940s Jewish men and women served as a "fierce resistance" fighting the British government that had mandated Palestine. These resistance fighters fought for a cause in which they truly believed: a free and independent Israel at peace.

This novel salutes those "fierce" resistance fighters and their indomitable spirit.

Chapter 1

It was now or never, Yitzy Gamel decided.

The satchel he carried was loaded with dynamite, fuses and gunpowder. At 0200 he and his buddy, Avram, sneaked down to the beach in Bat Yam and in the dark surprised two British sentries on routine patrol. The sentries' holstered revolvers were no match for the lightning quick speed of the resistance fighters' hidden daggers which were used to quickly stab and slice up the two sentries. The fighters then went about their work, setting up the dynamite, laying out the fuses and connecting them. It was tedious, nerve-wracking work done in the dim moonlight. By 0300 they detonated their charges. This late night raid and attack in March, 1937 resulting in the deaths of two Brits was blamed on a fledgling resistance organization, the Irgun.

The incident was listed the next day's newspaper as the "Arab Revolt."

Eight months later, in November, the Irgun struck again —this time, in Jerusalem. Ten Arab citizens were killed.

The pace of the attacks quickened after this latest action.

Multiple attacks against Arab citizens and British policemen were carried out by Irgun resistance fighters for two months in April with the resulting loss of three lives. May saw no letup in Irgun activity when a policeman was killed in an attack on a bus on Hebron Road in Jerusalem, and three people were shot and fatally wounded in Haifa. Multiple attacks against Palestinian citizens were carried out by Irgun freedom fighters the following month. The newspapers noted that "some of the most heinous attacks since this campaign started were the ones that were committed against youngsters in an Arab market in Haifa." It was noted that "most of the attacks were bomb attacks with the occasional use of guns."

In the neighborhoods and side streets of Jaffa and Tel Aviv, Itzhak Gamel was a local hero, fighting for the resistance.

He wasn't always such a hero, and life certainly wasn't always easy, he recalled. His parents, Otto and Hannah, had been living with their three children in two rooms in Glukhov, near Kiev. News of the Russian Revolution and Civil War, and the pogroms they heard about taking place in Poland, Romania and Lithuania had convinced them that for their own safety it was time to leave their homeland and emigrate to Palestine.

They boarded the ship SS Ruslan, arriving in the Port of Jaffa on the 19th of December, 1919, part of the third wave of newcomers to make Aliyah.

Life was different for him here. When he first arrived he was a newcomer, adjusting to learning a new language and meeting and making new friends in school. Everyone called him Yitzy. After spending half his day in school, he tended the crops in a small plot of land that was assigned to his family by the newcomers' farmers' collective. Tonight, like the other nights this past week or so, he had the same dream. It was his Papa Otto, Mama Hannah, his brother Yaakov, and sister Hadassah that he dreamt about. Hazily, it seemed to him like it was happening right now but clearly it was in the past—about the time that they boarded the ship to make Aliyah. It was a cold night. Papa was dressed in a heavy coat and boots, carrying two tattered suitcases. Mama was similarly dressed. They were walking up a ship's gangplank. Yitzy's little sister, Hadassah, age 6, whom they called Dassi, was crying. It looked like Mama was doing everything she could to keep Dassi quiet while she walked her up the gangplank to board. His younger brother, Yaakov, age 8, was carrying an old suitcase that was far too heavy for him. But where was he in the dream? He could sense a rising panic and started to yell out "Papa, Papa!" Then he would wake up. The memories from the past and his youth all revolved around his Papa.

The family moved and settled in Tel Aviv. Two years after making Aliyah, Otto, working in a jewelry wholesaler, was killed in a car accident in downtown Tel Aviv. At the funeral and the Shiva, Yitzy cried for his Papa for what seemed like hours on end. He knew that he was crying for himself as well. For he recalled the many ways he was like his Papa or tried to emulate him.

Yitzy was built like him, tall and skinny, had an oily complexion and some pimples. And he had a great smile and sense of humor. He would crack jokes at himself and found that he easily made new friends in school.

Yitzy's Bubbe, Rebekkah, passed away in Palestine soon after she and her husband, Moses, had emigrated to Palestine, which was two years after Otto and Hannah and the family had made the same journey. Over these years Zayde truly became part of the extended family. It was Zayde who helped Yitzy to learn and practice his prayers and it was Zayde who threw fly balls when his grandson, Yitzy, wanted to practice ball. Even though he knew his Zayde wouldn't live forever, Yitzy was shocked and speechless when the family was called by the hospital on a Thursday afternoon and told the news that Zayde had suffered a heart attack. Hannah took a taxicab to the hospital and was there with her father when he passed away. That just happened last year.

It was a very sad time in the Gamel house. Someone so close and dear to everyone in the family had been taken. It seemed so unfair. Yitzy seemed so sad, his mama noticed. He felt that he wanted to scream at the heavens and ask "why?" It was evident that this young man had known a lot of grief in his life at a young age.

But there were happy moments, too. Yitzy's bar mitzvah was a reason to celebrate. Hannah had arranged for a beautiful and meaningful Torah service and small kiddush afterwards one Shabbat morning, the first of September.

And the high school years were a time of friendships, first love and the path to a meaningful career. Yitzy was outgoing and had many friends. People found that he was easy to talk to, and in any group he stood out. He was level-headed, and in any situation he tried to see the other person's point of view.

It was early in his freshman year, at a pep rally, when Yitzy met Suzy Gershwitz. She was one of the rally organizers— small, petite, with lots of energy, a big smile, a quick brain and with the mouth to match. Yitzy smiled first, extended his hand and said, "Hi, I'm Yitzy Gamel."

"Hi, I'm Suzy Gershwitz," she replied, shaking Yitzy's hand ever so gently.

They quickly became a couple, and after their introductions to each other they found that they had similar tastes in radio programs, books and movies to see at the cinema. They became practically inseparable. The next three years of high school flew by for Yitzy and Suzy. They tried to get to the movies on an almost weekly basis even though money was scarce. Clark Gable, Spencer Tracy, Bette Davis and Joan Crawford movies were some of their particular favorites.

They both knew, but didn't want to admit, that their romance wouldn't go on after high school graduation. Suzy knew that her Mom couldn't afford to pay for her college courses, so she resigned herself to completing her education with a high school diploma and talked about it with Yitzy.

Yitzy had his own thoughts about the future. He had participated in the debate club in school and found that he enjoyed taking a position and defending it. Over these past six months he had many opportunities to debate other students and see first-hand other points of view. He thought about pre-law and law programs, even though they weren't considered a "major" subject in the university's curriculum. Yitzy had applied to Hebrew University and had been accepted for the law program. He was assigned a faculty advisor who met with him to help him map out his academic program and his schedule of classes. Because Palestine was a British mandated territory, Yitzy knew that he would be studying British law. He knew that he would also be studying constitutional and administrative law, principles of criminal law, contract law, the English legal process, and fundamentals of a legal practice. He found the subject of law fascinating, but quickly realized that the reading and homework load were going to be immense and figured that, for the foreseeable future, his free time was going to be spent in the school library. He estimated that it would take him three years to complete his studies and obtain a law degree. He also knew that he would have to stop a tendency to put things "off." His Mama reminded him that he had to "buckle down" and do the daily work required. No delays or excuses any more.

It was a Wednesday morning, early in the semester, when Yitzy's pal in the debate club, Moshe, saw him in the student cafeteria and said, "I'd like you to meet some new friends of mine."

Being a new student and anxious to make new friends, Yitzy said, "Yeah, sure, I want to meet them. When?"

Moshe was evasive, and kidding with his friend, he said, "You'll just have to wait and find out." And he gave Yitzy a teasing "nudge." The next afternoon, Moshe and Yitzy took the #4 bus to downtown Tel Aviv and walked the two blocks to the union workers hall. Once inside the hall, Moshe spotted a tall, swarthy man whom he recognized, and walked over to him. They shook hands and had a brief, animated discussion before Moshe walked back to where Yitzy was standing and made the introductions. "Yitzy, this is Mendel. Last names are not important here. You two should get to know each other." That was all that Moshe said, but Mendel's manner and business-like way made a definite impression on Yitzy.

After this brief introduction Yitzy and Moshe got into Mendel's car. Little was said as Mendel drove to the harbor-port area, parked on Dizengoff Street, and started walking.

"This view of the Mediterranean is terrific," Yitzy commented as he and the others walked to the pier a few blocks away. Yitzy didn't know that he was being photographed and would be unobtrusively followed and photographed for the next three days. Mendel knew where he was going. He stopped at a small restaurant on the wharf that didn't seem busy. The waitress recognized him and seated him and his party at a small booth in the back when they first came in. It was as if Mendel knew her, but that was crazy, he thought. The waitress hurried along the remaining diners and, by 6 pm, they were the only diners left in the restaurant and the waitress made herself scarce.

Mendel said, "Sorry for the secrecy but we have to be careful. You've been recommended for membership in our organization, Irgun Zvai Leumi." He added, "I am Mendel Weitz, a member coordinator. I cover the Tel Aviv district, specifically Hebrew University." Mendel stood up, walked over to where Yitzy was seated, extended his hand and shook hands with him. The "ice" was broken. For the next hour and a half Mendel talked at length and in depth about the organization and their stated goal of ridding Palestine of British rule. By force, when necessary.

This meeting was so great, Yitzy thought, brutally open and honest. He couldn't remember any other meeting he heard about where the subject of Palestine and British annexation had been covered so frankly. On the bus ride back from this meeting Yitzy and Moshe were very quiet, thinking about what had been said and what they had heard. Yitzy found himself intrigued and excited about the organization, the Irgun. He remembered what Mendel told him. "There is much to learn and do in the Irgun for men and women like yourself. This is just the beginning for you."

Yitzy asked Mendel about further contact and smiled broadly when Mendel said, "You'll definitely hear from me soon." And true to his word, Mendel had written a letter of welcome and confirmation to him that he was now a member of Irgun Zvai Leumi and arranged to have the letter signed and delivered to Yitzy's dorm room, in a sealed envelope, later that evening. Two weeks later Yitzy received a letter from Mendel informing him that he was to attend a required indoctrination session on Wednesday, 20 February.

A bus arrived at 6 am. Twenty-five young recruits, including Yitzy, and two section leaders, boarded the bus bound for a large kibbutz in Haifa that the Irgun was using for training and orientation. After the one hour trip, the recruits exited the bus. They then lined up alphabetically by last name. It was assumed that these recruits would be assigned to the Hayil Kravi, the combat corps. The next four hours were spent on formations, marching and drill exercises. Lunch was followed by map reading and an address by Chaim Ovitz, an Irgun Section Leader. As twilight descended on the field, the combat corps were practicing their drill exercises and maneuvers in the darkness. Six o'clock saw a lot of weary recruits board the bus to return home.

This mission was deemed a success and reported to the Irgun district commander. There would be many more missions for the combat corps.

Yitzy was happy to see some action, but he realized after the drill that he was very sore and out of shape. Like Yitzy, most of those who worked for the resistance held regular jobs and worked for the Irgun on a part-time basis.

Time seemed to move at a snail's pace for Yitzy. It was almost a year later. He found that he was spending three to four evenings each week in the school library. Often another student would have to wake him up from dozing while he was supposed to be reading. He often took notes late at night after class, but the following day the notes he wrote seemed like gibberish. He was always tired. There were too many courses and laws and tests. He felt that his vision seemed to be getting worse from all of the reading that he was doing. It wasn't just the classes as much as it was the required reading that he had to complete for each course. So far, he had completed his course work and reading for constitutional and administrative law, with a grade of B-, had completed the English law process with a grade of B, and had completed the fundamentals of a legal practice with a grade of B-.

He knew that the most formidable courses, in other words the ones in which he had the most interest, namely criminal law and contract law, were still to be taken in the upcoming term. He asked about the best way to study for the law classes and was told by a friend that study groups are the best way. "I happen to know that the Tuesday-Thursday law study group has an opening," his friend, Albert indicated. As Yitzy soon found out, joining a study group, especially an existing one, was not as easy as it would seem to be. For in the span of three weeks, he had called three times, had written multiple notes, and had even walked over to the student union and tacked a note up on the message board about the law class study group, but to no avail. A student named "M. Baum" was proving impossible to reach, either by written note or repeated phone calls. It was discouraging.

At 11 pm on a Thursday evening, Yitzy thought that he would try calling once more before going to sleep. A sleepy sounding young lady answered the phone on the second ring. "Hello," she said.

"Hi, I'm Itzhak Gamel," Yitzy said. "But my friends call me Yitzy. I've been trying to reach you."

"Yes, hi. I know. I'm Miriam Goldbaum. I'm sorry. I know you tried to reach me these past few weeks, but had no luck. I've been out of town taking care of my Mother, " she added. She sounds nice, he thought. "If I understand your bulletin board posts, you want to join our Tuesday-Thursday legal study group. Is that right?" Miriam asked.

"Yes, that's right," Yitzy answered. "Asked like a true lawyer," he added, jokingly. Miriam didn't answer him. Maybe she didn't hear me, he thought, and let it drop.

"Well, we do have the opening in our 'Legal' study group," Miriam said.

"Good. I'll take it."

"We meet every Tuesday and Thursday at six o'clock in conference room A in the library building," she said. "Bring your textbooks and note paper and a pen."

Brief and to the point—and that's that, he thought. At least I got into the study group. The next day was Thursday. Yitzy was looking forward to meeting Miriam and the other students in the study group. At five thirty the next evening, Yitzy crossed the campus and arrived at the door to conference room A shortly before 6 o'clock. The study group students drifted in by 6:15, and Miriam was one of the last students to arrive, Yitzy noticed. She was short and petite with long black hair flowing down her back.

She was near-sighted and spoke with a soft voice. But what you immediately noticed was her smile. She had a way of putting others at ease and a wonderful smile that seemed to brighten up the room and everyone in it. But not now. Miri felt the weight of everything going on in her life and felt that she needed to be the one to be cheered up. The study session went well and Yitzy did well, participating fully. After the session, Miri asked Yitzy to join her for a cup of coffee in the student union café.

Everyone always said that Miri was a "human dynamo." "I'm usually energetic," she told Yitzy, as they were sipping their coffees. "I am usually filled with a lot of energy, great at organizing a meeting or an event, and I'm always the most enthusiastic person in the room," she added. "But not lately, because my Mother has been really ill. It was unexpected," she added.

"You can't plan for something like that," Yitzy commented.

"My mother's illness really upset me. I'm sorry to burden you with my sad story, Yitzy." Miri reached her hand out and squeezed Yitzy's hand.

"I'm sorry about your Mother. How is she feeling?" he asked her, as he saw the tears welling up in Miri's eyes. It must be serious, he thought. Miri took a deep breath and said, "My mother has cancer and it's terminal." And then she cried. Yitzy gave her a hug and his handkerchief. A few minutes passed while Miri collected herself. Yitzy got her a glass of cold water. It was clear that Miri wanted to talk about her mother and share her feelings with Yitzy. She said, almost wistfully, "I'm an only child."

"What about your father?"

"My father hasn't been in the picture for many years. He was abusive to my mother, Devorah, and liked his alcohol," she said.

"I'm sorry to hear this."

"The situation got unbearable."

"When you say it got unbearable, what do you mean?"

"My father smacked my mother with his hand."

"Smacked her? What happened then?"

"My mother and I moved out of our apartment and moved in with my Bubbe, my grandma Rebecca."

"And now, how are things?"

"Well, there's been peace and quiet and happiness ever

since. But that's all changed with my mother's cancer."

"I imagine it's been tough for you."

"Yes, it's been tough, especially on Mama. It's the radiation treatments she's been getting that have been the hardest," Miri added. "But we deal with it."

Everyone who knew Miri and her family saw that once the family settled in with Bubbe, things improved. They were there for each other and they would handle whatever came their way with courage and optimism.

Miri's mood improved. She was her old buoyant self.

A month later, after one of the most lively study sessions that Miri could remember, Yitzy and Miri stopped in the student cafeteria for a cup of coffee. This had quickly become one of the rituals that they both looked forward to, sharing coffee and a spirited discussion with some of the other session group members. Tonight's session was no exception. The discussion was organized by Miri. The subject was "tort law-negligence"and the elements of a negligence case: duty, breach of duty, causation and damages. Each student took an element of tort law, explained what it meant and gave an example.

"I'm very impressed with the work you did today to put this together," Yitzy said to Miri.

He hung around after the session ended, smiling, but not saying anything. It was obvious that he had something on his mind.

"Yitzy, do you have something you want to say to me?" Miri asked. She had secretly been wanting Yitzy to ask her out the first time they met in the cafeteria. He had been so kind and gentle and solicitous when she told him about her mother. But Yitzi didn't say anything. He just let this opportunity go by.

Like most of Miri's friends, he didn't dwell on Miri's mother's condition any more and she was just as glad that they didn't, because her mother's health and condition were declining faster and faster. It was now just a matter of time, Miri thought.

Her mother passed away two weeks later.

What few knew was that Yitzi and Miri had gone out alone three times, and found that they really had enjoyed each other's company.

A simple funeral was held with Rabbi Auslander of Temple Torah officiating. Devorah was buried in a plain pine box. They all got through the funeral and the Shiva. Yitzi was there for Miri every step of this sad journey. He gave her comfort and support and proved to be a true "Mensch." Also, he helped Miri by coordinating the arrangements with the Rabbi. After the thirty-day period of mourning had passed, Yitzy and Miri surprised everyone by announcing their engagement and planned wedding in May.

During this hectic time Yitzy stayed as involved as he ever did in the work of the Irgun. A new branch of the Irgun had been formed in Jerusalem and he was deeply involved.

Miri and Yitzy were now more in love than when they first met. Their marriage under the Chuppah in May by Rabbi Auslander with family and friends there was beautiful.

Yitzy completed his studies in law and received his bachelor's degree and his JD degree and opened his legal practice on Ben Yehuda Street in Jerusalem the following year before the High Holidays. He also knew that it was time for him to use his given name all the time. So from now on to family, friends and business associates, he was known as Itzhak Gamel.

Chapter 2

Sometimes late at night, in the quiet of his law office on Ben Yehuda Street in downtown Jerusalem, Itzhak Gamel would take a break from his paperwork. He looked at the clock on his desk. It was 1:30 am, 5 April, 1946. He curled up on the two seat client couch and closed his eyes.

It was half an hour later. Itzhak went into the bathroom and splashed his face with cold water, and again he checked his watch—a little after two. It was late enough, he thought, as he returned back to his desk, put some case work in his briefcase and left the building. There was always parking behind the office building and, after this long day, Itzhak was happy to get inside his '40 Ford Coupe and head home.

His wife, Miriam, was fast asleep, so he quietly changed.

It seemed like he had just gotten into bed and pulled the covers up when the alarm rang on the nightstand. 5:45 am.

Itzhak showered and dressed. A quick toast and jam, and he headed to his car for the drive over to the office.

In his mind he reviewed his appointment calendar for the

day. Since his practice was a "local" practice most of the cases he would see would be general law cases—a complicated will to work through, a tenant/landlord dispute and a few telephone calls to be placed before the end of the day and his work with the Resistance. Itzhak knew that his cell, the Ben Yehuda Fighters, would meet promptly at 6 pm, whether he was there to start it or not. It was 5:15—he was running late. He hurried quickly to get to the tobacco warehouse.

Most days that was the routine. He would leave his car parked behind the office building, take the stairs from his second floor office, walk out the door and over to the bus stop two blocks away. The bus ride was quick. No one paid much attention to him as they were headed home from work. He tried not to look anybody in the eye. The less they focused on him the better, he thought.

It was a beat-up old wood door that led to the room in the back. The ceiling was low—you had to duck under exposed beams and rusted nails before you made it inside.

"Hello, Itzhak." It was Ari. He always came a little early. He liked to talk to the others, hearing what they had to say. Like many of the others, he worked in the fields after class. And then, like the others, he would get on the bus or hitch a ride to the warehouse. Itzhak looked around the room— crates and barrels were scattered. The musty smell of stale tobacco hung in the air. Straight back cane chairs were set up in rows of four and five. Men were coming in, greeting each other. Most of them were older; a few of them seemed to be around 22 or so. He could tell by their clothes—some were farmers, some were students, straight from school. And then there were a few dressed in their business suits. It was a little after 6 now. Itzhak strode into the room and silently sat down facing the others. He was small in stature; couldn't have been taller than 5'2" or so. You could tell by looking at him that he was a learned man—a scholar. At first glance he looked to be in his mid-forties. He was soft-spoken, and when he spoke you had to lean in to hear him. His suit was rumpled, his gray hair was wind-blown and there were deep creases in his face, probably from worries over money. "Let's get started. We have a lot to talk about," he said.

Itzhak looked around the room at the dozen or so seated there. Just about everyone was nodding in agreement. And then, just like every other time, as if by clockwork, the men stopped talking, grabbed chairs, arranged them in a semi-circle facing Itzhak and sat, waiting expectantly. The first half-hour was always devoted to status updates. To some of the men seated, this talk seemed to drone on and on. How many men were on security patrol, how many new recruits … and so on.

"BEN … BENJAMIN!" Itzhak's voice roused Benjamin Yosef out of his daydream.

"Yes. Sorry," Benjamin replied.

Itzhak glared at him for a moment and said "As one of our younger members, what are your thoughts?" he asked.

Benjamin looked around the room. Everyone had turned to look at him. Most of the younger men gave him a smile or at least an understanding look. The older men looked at him with disdain.

"Talk! Talk! I'm so sick and tired of talk," Benjamin said, and he sat down.

Itzhak stopped, walked over to where Benjamin was seated and, in a very soft, measured voice, said, "You have something to say, Ben. That's why we meet. Let the others know how you feel."

"Forget it. I have nothing important to say. Just more

talk, that's all," he replied.

Daniel wouldn't let it go. He stood up, spun around to face Benjamin and said, "Stop pretending, Benjy. Tell them what's been on your mind for so long. You know you've got friends here." There was murmuring amongst the others in the room until Itzhak crossed to the center of the room and said "We've given you every opportunity to speak, Ben. At every meeting …"

Benjamin stood up and cut Itzhak off. "—I know, Itzhak. I know what you're going to say. That I just sit at these meetings and don't say anything. Maybe I've been waiting and hoping …" And then, as if he were making an important speech to a bunch of professors, Benjamin walked to the center of the room, put his hand up to gain everyone's attention, and said, "Itzhak and my fellow members of the Resistance, I am sick and tired of coming to every meeting and hearing talk. We have talked and talked and talked. We have heard each other's bitter feelings. But not just once. Every time we come we hear about the cruelty of the Nazis, the evils of the British. Was that why we came together? To talk?" he asked.

Everybody seemed to respond all at once—then one of the newer members, Yonkel, said, "You talk about everybody else's bitter feelings …. Well, how about yours?"

Benjamin could feel his face turning crimson with anger. He waited for a few moments to collect his composure and then said, "Let me finish what I've started. It seems to me that we'll continue to meet each week and do nothing but talk. When do we get the British occupiers out of Palestine? Will we get them out of our land by talk? We should be acting now … The only way the British will be removed will be with our fists … and our guns. Not by someone's bitter feelings left over from the War."

It didn't take long for Itzhak to respond, "You're such a child, Ben. You think it's so simple. We just fire pistols and the British leave. Is that what you think? he asked.

"No, that's not what I mean," Benjamin replied, as loudly and forcefully as he could.

Itzhak stopped and seemed to glare at Benjamin.

"You don't understand me, Itzhak," Benjamin said. He added "We plan very carefully. We attack something like the supply fortress at Ramat Gan. If we're prepared we can easily outmaneuver them." Everyone stopped and waited to see what Itzhak would do.

Nothing dramatic took place. Instead, Itzhak turned and slowly walked to the front of the room and said, "No, forget that idea, Benjamin. That supply fortress is well-guarded. Almost one-quarter of all British arms are kept there. Our men don't have the training to defeat the British and capture their arms. Don't forget—we're only one of many cells. Maybe in a few months we'll be ready for action on a smaller scale. We must build up our strength and plan carefully before we can do something so bold as attack a fortress. To go into an action like that now would mean nothing short of a massacre," he added.

"And what of our families, Itzhak? Don't you think our families deserve a better way of life … better treatment than they are getting, living in a land occupied by foreigners?" Benjamin asked.

"Now look, Ben," Itzhak replied. "I'm thinking of our families when I say we have to wait. We're not trained fighters. And it isn't just our cell. We have to coordinate with the others. If we rush into action blindly—it's going to mean lots of us in a battle we're not prepared to fight."

"You talk like a coward," Benjamin replied. "Are you afraid to die?"

"Afraid? It isn't that simple," Itzhak answered. "There are so many factors that have to be considered. You're not being realistic, Ben."

The growing anger that each man exhibited reached the point where Itzhak and Benjamin just stood there silently glaring at each other for a few minutes. It was clear that the dialogue wasn't over. Benjamin crossed to the back of the room and stood there, waiting to see what would happen next. He didn't have to wait long. Within a few minutes most everyone turned their chairs completely around so that they were facing him.

Benjamin said, "I say to each of you, sitting here and listening to me, that the longer we wait to take arms against the occupation government, the less our chances will be to defeat them and see the Free State." He saw eyes opening widely … they were listening! "Every day the British propaganda fills the mind of another Jew, turning him against us and wooing him to their point of view. Every day we wait, more British soldiers enter our land," Benjamin noted. "The Resistance counter-attack must begin now if there is ever to be a free state," he added.

Much murmuring and shouts from the men sitting there convinced him that what he said was what most were thinking but hadn't expressed their feelings verbally. Benjamin sat down, feeling a mix of euphoria and dread. He knew that he had to take a stand and now he had.

Itzhak ran over to where Benjamin was sitting. He

pointed his finger at him, actually waving it at him in a disapproving way, saying, "You're living in a dream world, Ben. You're a child who has been given a weapon and your fingers itch. They itch for action—you're anxious to pull that trigger. You do, and face a war which we're not ready to fight. Grow up!"

"Grow up? What the hell does that mean?" Benjamin asked.

Itzhak seemed to get angrier than he had been. He inched in closer to Benjamin's face, saying, "Just what I said…Grow up…and realize that when the time is right, we'll be there. I want the British out of our land as much as you do…and so does everybody else here. But I can't see risking our lives now." And then, almost as an afterthought as he sat down in his chair, Itzhak said, "Heaven help you if you try to start this on your own. You'll be in a grave at a very early age."

Benjamin stood up. He looked at no one in particular but knew that he had to get out. His legs seemed to carry him out without even thinking about it. Once he got out and was back in the street, it was night. Benjamin knew he had to walk. And think. What now? He knew he couldn't let it go….he just knew.

In the tobacco warehouse a few minutes later, Itzhak wrapped up the meeting with a "Good Night" and "Shalom." A few stayed a little longer just to chat. Itzhak walked around the room, pulling the strings to turn off the overhead lights. As he usually did after the meeting broke, he headed down to the bus stop to go back to his office. On the short walk to the bus stop, and then on the bus, Itzhak had a chance to think about the meeting. Clearly, he was worried that youthful impatience might spiral his plans for the cell out of control.

There was not much that he could do, he thought, as he

walked to his car and drove home. On the twenty-minute drive home for dinner with Miriam, Itzhak thought about his involvement with the Resistance. When his family first arrived in Jerusalem, his Hebrew was poor. Along with many others, he went to a school for newcomers for part of the day.

And then in the afternoon he worked in the fields. A lot of the planting of the crop and harvesting of the wheat was done by hand. Itzhak didn't bring home much money, but whatever he brought he gave to his mother. Papa didn't work. He sat in the front room and either read or listened to music on the radio or napped. He had been a skilled carpenter, but there were no jobs.

It was at the fields where Itzhak met Avraham. They called him Avi. Like so many of the other newcomers, Itzhak learned about the struggle for a free Palestine from his friends in school. He would hear them talk about the resistance movement—the fight for a homeland for the Jews. Avi knew a lot, and patiently answered Itzhak's questions. He said to Itzhak, "Come down to a meeting. We meet weekly—more when we need to. We need good men like you." Itzhak remembered that first meeting. Everyone seemed so friendly. Some older men, some his age. They asked him to stand up and tell them who he was. He did. They clapped, shook his hand, patted him on the back, and let him know that he was welcome. In the meeting the men talked about the newly organized resistance group called "Haganah." One of his new friends, Shmuel, explained to Itzhak and the others at one of their regular Tuesday night meetings that local Arab gangs had been attacking Jews. "Now look," Shmuel said, "the Brits are running our government but they're not doing anything to protect us."

"So what have we been doing to protect our farms and Kibbutzim?" another member, Daniel, asked.

"We have been taking turns watching each other's lands," Shmuel explained. "And warning each other when Arabs try to attack."

This is where I belong, Itzhak thought the first time he went. He had new friends and a purpose.

He went every week, usually after working the fields. He didn't come to any conclusions right away. He sat and listened to the meetings every week. What he gathered by listening to the others in the meeting was that he and his fellow Resistance members were using the threat of violence or actually carrying out violent acts to get what they wanted— political change.

The term he heard Avi and the others use to describe this was "terrorism."

When he first heard it, Itzhak was taken aback. Is this what he joined for? To threaten or actually hurt people or property? After he sat and thought about it, in his heart and mind Itzhak knew that he needed to be a part of this Resistance movement.

The horn of a car behind him took him out of his daydreaming.

After nearly thirty years of life in Palestine and his close personal involvement all of those years with the Jewish Resistance movement, Itzhak felt that he was always on shaky ground. From the pogroms in Europe in 1919 when he and his family first emigrated, through the Western Wall uprising, the horrors of the Holocaust, the ongong animosity with the Arabs and the Brits, he always steeled himself for the unexpected event ready to happen at any moment. And, of course, there were plenty of times when Itzhak wondered what he was doing mixed up in all of this. He brushed aside these thoughts for the moment, anyway, as he turned off the car engine and went inside for dinner. As Itzhak finished his dinner and sipped his tea, he sat, deep in thought. His wife Miriam knew that sometimes when he was troubled or needed to solve work through issues he couldn't talk to Miri about, he would sit at the kitchen table, rest his head on his arm, and seem to fall asleep. Tonight was one of those nights.

He knew that Palestine was a "powder keg" at this time. Besides the Haganah, other militant groups had sprung up. The Lehi (Fighters For The Freedom of Israel), the Stern Gang and and his organization, Irgun Zvai Leumi, were seeing young, impressionable men—and some women—showing up at their meeting sites. Some who came were not sure why. But it was clear to Itzhak that most of the young people were coming because they wanted to "belong," to have an identity, to feel that they were needed.

Daily news over the radio painted a bleak picture of a constantly unsteady, useasy place where bombings, shootings, and significant violence had become a regular part of life. Would things ever get easier, Itzhak wondered to himself, as he settled into bed. He leaned over, gave Miri a kiss, and tried to sleep.

Benjamin couldn't let it go. He was so angry he could taste the bile in his throat. Images and words from the meeting earlier in the day were running around in his head as he walked down the street, crossed over one block and then the other, until he was standing at the bus stop. As he stood waiting for the bus home, he thought, "How dare he!" When Itzhak sat there in that meeting and accused Benjamin of looking to start a war against the Brits on his own, he was so mad. With more time to think, to stew about it some more as he looked down the street for the damn bus which never seemed to come quickly, he thought to himself, "I know how I feel. This is our land. The Brits don't have any reason to be here," he muttered out loud to no one in particular. People waiting for the bus were staring back at him but he didn't care.

You know how the mind works? In an instant Benjamin was remembering 1940. His family was living in a two-bedroom apartment in Warsaw then. Benjamin, age 14, his Papa, Yechiel, and his brother, Moshe, age 12, slept in one bedroom. His mother, Sarah, and sister Rebecca, age 6, slept in the other bedroom. The bathroom, used by everyone on the floor, was in the hall. Benjamin had undergone a growth spurt. He was tall, skinny and had red hair and freckles. His oily skin and acne were a constant source of embarrassment to him. Benjamin tried his best not to pick at the pimples but they constantly seemed to itch. His face had pockmarks, too. It certainly didn't help him to meet girls, he thought. Here in Warsaw everybody was going about their daily lives, but deep inside there was an unspoken but ever-present fear of the Nazis and what they might do. No one seemed to know what might happen next.

Over breakfast one morning, Mama told her children that there was talk of forcing them to pack and move to a place where the Jews would have to live in a crammed space. The thought was terrifying. And then, a couple of weeks later, the notice came. Their papa would be going to a work camp in a place called Treblinka, fifty miles outside of Warsaw.

Papa was a watchmaker by trade. No work at the shop changed that. When he was a young man, Yechiel loved to work on the farm. He shared stories with the family about helping his Papa work the farm in Lodz. Their Papa knew hard work but now, an older man, he had to dig ditches to put some food on the table. Their mother, Sarah, who loved to visit with the neighbors and listen to the music on the radio, stopped going out and liked to sit quietly in the front room of the dimly lit apartment. She watched neighbors' children and would accept whatever money or food they would give her in return. Less than a month later, their Papa was on a train. He left early in the morning before Becca was awake. He went into the room where she was sleeping to say goodbye. He spoke a few words to each of his children, shook Benjamin's hand, and rubbed the hair away from in front of Moshe's face. He kissed Mama and gave her a hug. There were tears in Mama's eyes and in Papa's too, because deep down they both knew that they would never be together again.

Sarah didn't talk much anymore about when Papa would be coming home. She didn't have to....

A few months passed before Sarah got word through a Jewish relief organization that the family had qualified to relocate to an apartment in Palestine. Sarah told Rebecca and the boys that where they were going might not be as nice as where they were living now but at least they would all be together and safer and that they would manage. Sarah packed the few things the family owned in some cardboard boxes and they travelled—first by train, and then by a transport ship. The trip was long and tiring. After three days they arrived in Jerusalem,

It was early 1940, and Sarah knew how fortunate they were to be out of Poland. If they had remained then they might have been headed for the ghetto or worse.

Like so many others before them, Benjamin, Rebecca and Moshe went to Newcomers' School for a portion of the day until they had learned Hebrew. The rest of the time they attended public school. Benjamin also worked a few hours in the afternoons on a kibbutz on the outskirts of Rosh Pinah. He usually rode the bus from downtown Jerusalem to get there. It was in school where Benjamin first heard about the Resistance. He heard about the Haganah and the Irgun, who were not only carrying out attacks against Palestinian Arabs, but were also attacking British soldiers. The use of violence against civilians to rid Palestine of the Brits and lead to a free state for the Jews seemed like a really good thing to Benjamin. Spirited arguments with his school friends, sometimes going into the evening, became a great way to spend time and make friends. Inevitably, the conversations led to talk about the Resistance.

Benjamin felt that it would only be a matter of time until he got mixed up in it and the prospect seemed to excite him. Over the last four or five months or so, an offshoot of an existing cell, the Ben Yehuda Fighters, had started up. They were meeting in an old tobacco warehouse near Ben Yehuda Street in downtown Jerusalem. Through a friend of his friend, Chaim, Benjamin received a handwritten note to come down to the warehouse. It was a brisk afternoon, 10 February, 1945.

Benjamin had been careful not to say anything about where he was going after his shift at the Kibbutz. He boarded the bus that left him off two blocks from the old warehouse. He met his friend Chaim, who walked with him up to the entrance. Once inside, Benjamin met the cell leader, Itzhak Gamel, and once the meeting started, he was introduced to the group. Itzhak made it a point to introduce Benjamin warmly. Everyone that Benjamin met that evening seemed so friendly, giving him pats on the back, handshakes, and showing real interest in him and what he had to say. He really liked the men who came to this first meeting that he attended. Many of them were students in school, some were farmers, and there were a few clerks.

Conversations were spirited. Everyone had an opinion.

For Benjamin, that was the way it had been for all of the meetings he attended until last week's meeting and the verbal confrontation with Itzhak. Benjamin knew in his heart and mind that sitting around in a meeting wasn't enough. He was arguing with friends in school. He was a little jumpy with Moshe and Becca. Sometimes the anger and frustration of it all would burn so that he could feel his heart racing and his skin would be clammy. When he got home, Benjamin decided that the less he said to Mama, Moshe or Becca, the better. They had gotten used to him sometimes coming home from the fields and going directly to my bed without saying a word. The next day would be time enough.

It was a Tuesday morning. As usual, Benjamin was the first one up. He got dressed quickly, had a quick bread and jam and then made a phone call to his friend Hirschl. Benjamin asked Hirschl to meet him in front of the apartment in a half-hour.

That's all that he would tell him, so Hirschl knew that something was up. Benjamin took one last look around the apartment, realizing that this might be his last chance to be with Mama or his family for a while and he headed off.

A half hour later Hirschl came by. There, in the back of the apartment buildings, there was a patio where the mothers and their children played in the sun. At this time of the morning, they were the only ones there.

"What's with all the mystery, Ben?" Hirschl asked.

Benjamin looked at him and, speaking in a low voice, said, "I thought about this long and hard, Hirsh. Look, the Brits have no business in what should be our homeland."

Hirschl listened, nodding his head. "I want to send a message to the Brits. And I need your help," Benjamin said.

"Sure, Ben. What can I do?" Hirschl replied. Benjamin leaned into him very closely and said, "You know that pistol you have at home. Well I need it. That and a lift to the Fort at Acre."

Hirschl lost the smile that he was wearing just a few moments ago, tightened his jaw, and gulped. He looked at Benjamin in a hard way. He thought to himself, Why, he's a kid like me. What the hell are we doing? Hirschl shook that thought off. "All right, Ben," he said. "I'll go home and get it. Be back in about twenty." They shook hands. Hirschl got into his car and drove away.

It wasn't a kid's game anymore. Suddenly things had become more serious. True to his word, Hirschl was back in less than twenty. He had an old knapsack with him that he wore over his shoulder. Benjamin assumed it was the gun. Hirschl handed the knapsack over and said "Here's the pistol." And as he passed it over, he asked Benjamin, "Do you even know how to use it?"

"I don't have a clue, Hirsch, and that's the truth. Let's go where we won't be seen." Benjamin and Hirschl walked over to the area where the building's trash is stored for pickup. Benjamin was careful to be sure that no one was watching. He slowly unzipped the knapsack and looked at the pistol as he pulled it out. It was an old silver pistol, small, with some rust on the barrel.

"Be careful. It's loaded," Hirschl said.

"What do I do?"

"Watch me," Hirschl replied. Hirschl took the pistol in his right hand, raised his arm until it was shoulder level, and then he said, "I can't fire it here. But when you're ready to use it just squeeze the trigger." Benjamin nodded in agreement. "Better put it away before someone comes along," Hirschl said. Benjamin put the gun back in the knapsack and zippered it up.

Just as he was finishing, one of the mothers was walking hand in hand with her daughter by the area where they were standing. Benjamin and Hirschl gave each other a nervous look and didn't move until they saw the mother and daughter walk away. They got into Hirschl's father's old Pontiac. His dad was OK with letting Hirsh drive as long as he didn't race the engine. They didn't say much as they drove. They glanced over at each other a couple of times but were really into their own thoughts.

The drive toward Acre took them along the Old Highway and the seashore but today they hardly even noticed. Within a half an hour they came to a quiet side street about a block and a half from the fort's entrance. Hirschl stopped the car and said, "We're here, Ben." Benjamin nodded, and as he turned to get out of the car, Hirschl asked him, "Do you need me to stay?"

Benjamin could feel his body starting to shake from excitement or fear or a combination of them but he shook it off and said, "No, Hirsch, you go. Thanks." They shook hands. Benjamin got out of the car, took the knapsack with the gun in it, and started walking down the road as he watched Hirschl drive off.

By this time traffic had picked up and he watched as cars whizzed by. Benjamin stood so that his back was facing the road. He unzipped the bag and took out the gun. He figured he would wait until he saw the right moment and then shoot. He didn't have to wait too long until he saw a large truck heading up the road about a mile or so away. It was green, had what looked like military markings (the Union Jack, maybe) on the doors, and a covered awning for soldiers to ride in the back. He waited until the truck was just passing by his position. His hand was shaking really badly and he thought he might have to use two hands to steady the gun. He tried to remember what Hirsh had told him about firing it. Quickly now, he thought.

He lifted the gun straight up in the air and pulled the trigger. "BOOM!" The force from the shot made his arm twist back. He could smell the gunpowder in the air. The sound of the shot echoed from the hill above.

Benjamin listened and looked as the brakes quickly stopped the truck and at least ten soldiers jumped out from the back.

He just stood transfixed and, in what seemed like a long time, but really wasn't, the soldiers surrounded him with their rifles pointed at him. One soldier, (probably a lieutenant or something like that, he thought), told Benjamin to drop the gun and get down on his belly. He did as he was told. They took his gun, put handcuffs on him, and marched him to the back of the truck. Soon soldiers sat surrounding Benjamin as the truck drove quickly to the fort.

Little was said to him until one of the Brit soldiers led him to a cell. The handcuffs were removed. The soldier told Benjamin to strip to make sure that he wasn't carrying any hidden arms or explosives and then he let him get dressed. Other than the clothes on his back, Benjamin's things were taken and he didn't see anybody for hours. Then, in a flurry of activity, Benjamin was brought to an interview room somewhere down below in the fort. There, a Sergeant, another officer and a government official talked to him. At first, the questions were basic ones: who he was, where he was from, and what was he doing.

Basically, other than his name and address, Benjamin didn't have anything more to add, and tried his best not to show any emotion. But that didn't stop them—especially the government official, from asking him questions in a rapid-fire delivery.

Benjamin didn't seem to react but only told them his name and address in a flat, unemotional way. When Benjamin was asked if he had anything to say, he responded by asking to see his lawyer, Itzhak Gamel. He knew that they couldn't deny him that.

Benjamin remembered what Itzhak once told the group at one of the weekly meetings—that if any one of them ever got into trouble with the authorities, the best thing to do would be to say little and get to him any way they could. It would be the next day before Itzhak Gamel was advised of Benjamin's capture and arrest. Once Itzhak was briefed, the members of the Ben Yehuda cell worked quickly and efficiently to gather as much information as possible. They wrote whatever information they could gather on the legal size yellow pads that Itzhak preferred to use in his law practice. Itzhak knew the difficult task that faced him.

First, he would have to advise the parents of Benjamin's arrest. In this troubled time, when incidents involving troubled young men with a pistol were on the rise, and shootings and bombings by resistance force members had become an almost every day occurrence, Itzhak, like many others, had become immune or insensitive to these jarring reminders of a changed society.

It wasn't always so, Itzhak remembered. In the 1920s, when he and Miri first met, they courted under the watchful eye of Miri's papa, Eliezer, who was very strict when it came to his youngest unmarried daughter. The "children," as they were called, had to be chaperoned at all times. They could not sit in the front parlor without being watched by Miri's mother or father.

Boy, he thought, how times have changed!

Chapter 3

S ybil Elizabeth Hargrove—that was the name on the
record of birth. She was the daughter of Edward and
Millicent Hargrove and was born on 12 April 1934 in
Croydon, England, a large town in South London,15.3 km
south of Charing Cross. Her father, Edward Junior (called
"Ted" by everyone), was an officer in the British Foreign
Service, assigned to the office of the High Commissioner of
British Mandatory Palestine. Her mother, Millicent, was a
housewife who had previously worked as a retail clerk in a
Croydon jewelry store. The birth of her daughter, Sybil, had
not been an easy one, and Millie had decided to take time off
after the birth.

For sure, Sybil had not been an easy child. As a baby she
was finicky, had colic and had to be bottle fed. Growing up,
she developed allergies, had terrible nightmares, and wouldn't
sleep in her own bed.

But the situation improved.

As she entered her teens, she had her first period, got
through puberty and developed a nice figure. Her parents and

her granny doted on her and were constantly buying her clothes from Harrod's and the other trendy stores in London. Then, two years ago, things changed. She vividly recalled when her Dad (Ted, to everybody but Granny), held a family meeting with her, her granny, and her Mum Millie.

Now Sybil knew that Dad worked for the British Government while her Mum stayed home. He was often travelling on home office "business." But this time things were different, she noted. Her Dad would be travelling to Palestine to help set up the "High Command" that would administer the provisional government under British rule. And that's all she knew. Her Dad wasn't one to mince words when he said to her and her Mum, "Look, I have to be there, and I need both of you with me. You're my family." What could she say? Even if she was asked, she knew that she had to go along. Sybil resigned herself to being glum. They packed and moved from their home. All of her school chums! And some very cute boys! Sybil wept—but what was the point?

Her Dad said that ancient saying "stiff upper lip," but she was blue and glum and would be for quite a while, she knew.

Her Mum and Dad had warned her about keeping up her grades in university and making the right effort in her studies.

And then there was the part-time job in the bookstore—2 until 6 most days, except for Friday night at Sundown and, of course, Saturday, when everything closed. She missed home—her real home and friends in Croydon.

Life was a bore in Jerusalem for Sybil—but then she met Moshe. He was 19, and he had come into the bookstore with a list of books he needed for University and recognized Sybil behind the register. He smiled at her in a very shy way. She found it charming. He had a boyish look, red hair and a nice physique, Sybil noted. He was tanned and had a little bit of stubble on his chin. Moshe smiled at Sybil as he wrote his phone number on a slip of paper that he passed over to her and said, "I've seen you at school and now here in the bookstore. I'm Moshe. I'd really like to get to know you better. Call me."

That night, in her bedroom, Sybil looked at herself in the mirror, turning this way and that. And, frankly, she liked what she saw. Her 5'5" frame looked good in her jumper and plaid skirt and her sensible flats. Pictures of Madeleine Carroll in *Modern Photoplay* gave her the idea for the upsweep, which complemented her brown hair and gave her a very sophisticated look. Most important to her, though, was that she was a "good" girl. Sybil didn't swear, didn't smoke cigarettes and wasn't too "fast" with the boys.

The idea to ring up a boy, especially one she just met, was very forward of Sybil, but she didn't care. The next day, before the afternoon began, Sybil called Moshe's home and left a message with his sister. "Please tell Moshe that Sybil from the Bookstore called, and to please call back." It didn't take long. Before the evening was over they spoke on the phone and agreed to meet the following day.

It went well. He asked Syb (as she liked to be called) about herself. He wanted to know everything. What food she liked to eat, what music she liked to hear, what London was like, what the schools are like over there. He was an incredible listener. "He would lean in and keep his gaze on you so you felt like no one else was in the room," she said.

Most evenings, after work, Sybil and Moshe would meet at the café near the bookstore. Nothing fancy to eat—just some rice and bread and some brown gravy, but most evenings they were just about the only ones in the shop after it closed. Most nights, there in the dark, behind the shop, they would have long, wonderful talks and kisses. Lots of kisses. And hugs. She would press herself against him and shiver so. They would talk about her family, about school, friends, her folks. He told Sybil that he was a Jew and was proud about it. He talked about the people in his family. "The feeling is so strong," he told her, "that sometimes I feel overwhelmed," he added. Sybil felt incredibly close to Moshe; closer than with anyone else.

After a few weeks of seeing him she knew she was in love.

Then, one night not that long ago, he got very serious. "Listen, Syb," he said. "I know you've been asking about my family and I keep giving you kind of a run-around. But I think you should know about them," he said.

It was after 8 pm and everyone in the store had already gone home. Sybil had a copy of the key to the back door to the store so she said to Moshe, "let's go into the back."

He sat down in the chair across from her in the rear courtyard behind the store. And then he told Sybil about his family.

"My father," he said, "died in a concentration camp." She looked at him for a moment and noticed that he swallowed hard as he said, "I still miss him." They were both quiet for a few moments. Then he continued. "My mother's done all she can to keep us all together. There's my brother, Benjy, and my sister Becca," he added.

"Are you close with them?"

"I guess so. My brother Benjy went to college and now he works in the fields."

"And your sister?"

Moshe smiled. "She's fourteen. She's a good kid. Not bratty. She's always been the little princess. And I love to tease her," he added.

"I hope to meet them sometime," Sybil said.

"Don't worry, you will," Moshe replied.

He knelt down beside Sybil, took her face in his hands and gently kissed it. It was a long, deep and sweet kiss. Sybil melted. She thought to herself that she hadn't gone all the way with any boy. But with Moshe it was different. She knew that she would be ready for him when he asked.

Another evening, not long ago, Moshe took on a very serious look and asked Sybil, "Have you told your parents about me?"

The question caught her off guard. Sybil quickly responded by saying, "I told my folks that I'm seeing someone. I kept it vague. I didn't tell them your name or that you're a Jew." Sybil knew that she wasn't good at lying, especially to her parents.

She only hoped that she could confide in her Mum before her Dad found out.

It was Friday afternoon in Jerusalem. Everyone was either at home, or on their way there to prepare for Shabbat. Moshe had come from school a half hour ago. His sister Rebecca had an early dismissal from high school on Friday so she was home helping her mother with the cooking and preparation for Shabbat dinner.

"Moshe, where is your brother," Sarah asked her son. "He hasn't come home yet and we're almost ready to light the candles."

Moshe quickly replied from the kitchen, "He said that he would be late coming from the market, Mama. He was hoping to sell most of the soybeans he had."

"He always seems to be late, especially before Shabbat," she added.

Moshe didn't respond. Instead he buried his face in the prayers.

Just as they were ready to begin their prayers before lighting the Shabbat candles, the doorbell rang. Incessantly.

"Go see who's at the door," Sarah said to her 14-year-old daughter Rebecca.

"Yes, Mama."

Rebecca went to the door. Sarah and Moshe could hear that she was talking to a man.

"Who is it, Rebecca?" Sarah asked.

"It's a Mister Gamel, Mama. He said he must talk to you right now."

Sarah stood up but didn't go to the door as she said, "Now? But it's Shabbat. Tell him to come back on Sunday."

"But Mama," Rebecca replied, "He said it's about Benjy. He's in some kind of trouble."

Sarah walked quickly to the hallway. A short man in a rumpled suit carrying a briefcase was standing there. "Yes?" Sarah said.

"I'm Itzhak Gamel. I'm an attorney. Your son Benjamin was arrested today," he said. Itzhak took his business card out of his wallet and gave it to her.

Sarah stared at him for a moment, then at his card, and then she said, "This cannot be. He works in the fields as a farmer. He goes to the market and sells our crops. He's there right now," she added.

"Look, Mrs. Yosef, Itzhak said. "I'm sorry that I have to be the person to tell you, but your son is a member of the Resistance. He has been for quite a while," he said.

Sarah stood stock still for a moment as though she was trying to comprehend what he was saying. And then she responded in a soft voice, "The Resistance? How do you know this? No, no, this cannot be...."

"It is," he replied. And then he continued to explain. "How do I know this? I know it because I'm a Liaison Officer in the Resistance. Our struggle continues for a free Palestine. I came to tell you that your son Benjamin is being held as a prisoner at the Fortress at Acre."

"How did this happen? What did he do?" she asked.

Itzhak responded firmly, "Now look, I can't tell you word-for-word just what he said. But he stood up in our last meeting...He was so angry. ....Said he wanted to see things happening faster...You know he feels like many of us do....He blames the Brits..."the occupiers," he calls them. I told him not to be too quick to act....to wait til we're ready. But you know Benjamin... headstrong, impulsive.... I tried warning him but he wouldn't listen to me."

Sarah shook her head as if to say no. "My Benjamin?...A member of the Resistance? "He's a fool... like his father was. In the work camp my Yechiel tried organizing a Resistance just like you're trying to.....They tortured him...And now, my son. My stupid, foolish son," Sarah said. Sarah's cries of anguish mixed with tears.

Itzhak stood and patiently waited until Sarah calmed down a bit and then he said, "Here's what I've been told. This morning Benjamin shot a rifle as some British soldiers were riding down the Rose Pinah Highway in a truck. That's the story that the Brits are handing out. I haven't had a chance to hear it officially or to meet with Benjamin myself, but I'm going to the prison tonight."

"Please.....What will they do to him?" Sarah asked pleadingly.

"It's kind of hard to say at this point. My guess is they'll put him on trial," he replied.

"Maybe I should go with you to the prison. Benjamin might need me," Sarah suggested.

But Itzhak quickly suggested otherwise. "I don't think you should come right now. More important I hear what happened from him. I also want to make sure that he's treated fairly," he said.

Sarah shook her head from side to side, moaning softly.

Itzhak said: "I'll let him know that your prayers and your love are with him."

Moshe went to Sarah's side and tried to comfort her. But she pushed him away, and in a scolding tone she said: "You knew, didn't you?" He didn't answer at first, but merely looked at her. But she wouldn't let it go and again asked him, "Answer me. You knew, didn't you?" And then she screamed at him, "DIDN'T YOU?"

What could he do? Moshe didn't want to lie any more. And so, in a very quiet voice, in deliberate, measured words he told Sarah, "He didn't want to worry you, Mama. He knew what Papa's death did to you and he didn't want to upset you every time he went to a Resistance meeting. It was something he had to do, Mama. That's what he told me. Many times he wasn't at the marketplace selling the crops. Instead, he was at the meetings. I did some of his work on the farm but couldn't tell you. He warned me not to worry you. He loves you, Mama. He didn't want to hurt you."

Sarah stared at her son for a few moments. She couldn't believe what was happening. Then Sarah said, "How am I supposed to feel now? Should I thank God for giving my son the privilege of being a prisoner? Should I be joyful that

Benjamin joined the Resistance movement without my knowledge? He is still such a child."

With just about his next breath Itzhak squarely faced Sarah and said, "No, he's a man. I know it's difficult for you to understand, Mrs. Yosef. You're probably asking yourself why men risk their lives, their jobs, their homes for a cause. My wife wonders all the time. Look, I don't have all the answers. All I know is, when a man has a dream, a dream that burns inside him day and night, he'll give up everything he has to see it through."

Then Sarah said, "But we need him, Mr. Gamel. We love him. Doesn't he still owe something to his mother, his brother, his sister?"

Itzhak knew exactly what he needed to say, "I know your Benjamin. I've listened to him at our meetings. He's so passionate, so idealistic. He feels he owes you and himself and his brothers and sisters of the Resistance a better way of life. A chance to live in peace in a free country. Whether he's right or wrong is not the main point. How he fights for a cause with such vigor and love....It's reason enough for any parent to thank Hashem for such a son."

Again Sarah started wailing and crying, " My Ben! My son! He'll die, he'll die. I know it, I know it, I know it. He'll die!"

With that Itzhak asked for his coat and hat. As he put them on he said to Moshe, "I'd better be going. I'll be in touch when I have more to tell you. Your Mother needs you now."

As he left he shook hands with Moshe, nodded to Rebecca, and acknowledged Sarah with a slight nod of his head and left.

The remainder of the evening was tough. Both Rebecca

and Moshe tried to calm Sarah down, but her crying didn't stop for long. When she did finally fall asleep, Sarah was exhausted.

Moshe knew he had to get out of the apartment. "I've gotta go out, Beck," he said to his sister. There was only one person who totally understood him. He needed to see Sybil.

The call from Moshe came in the evening. Sybil was surprised that he would be calling her during the Sabbath. Obviously something was wrong. Her Mum answered the phone and didn't ask a whole lot of questions, which was a good thing. He was emotional. It sounded like he had been crying.

"What? See you now? I don't see how it's possible," she answered. But Sybil knew it had to be serious, or else why would Moshe be calling her now? "Let me see what I can do," she answered, and hung up the phone.

Her Mum was in the kitchen preparing dinner and her Dad hadn't come home yet. "Mum, I need to help my friend with a class assignment so I have to go out now," she said.

"But Syb, it's almost dinner time and your Dad will be home soon."

More insistently, Sybil responded, "I have to go out and help my classmate, Mum. I'll be home in a little while." She grabbed her sweater from the hall closet in the foyer and was gone. The trip was one that Sybil was familiar with—one bus ride and a short walk over to the bookstore where she worked.

As she boarded the bus and sat down, Sybil thought about Moshe. In the past few months they had grown closer than ever. When they were apart, they wrote short notes to each other which they would keep until they were able to be together again, and then they would read each other's notes.

At school Sybil thought about Moshe all the time. Alone in her room, she wrote long entries in her diary about him. She pictured him working in the fields, his shirt open at the waist. She dreamed about him hugging her and kissing her with a warm and passionate kiss. Their schedules at school were different, so unless they had arranged it in advance, they wouldn't be able to meet. But they did meet for an hour or so at least two times during the week. They would sit next to each other in the study carrels. Moshe would playfully rub his stockinged feet on Sybil's leg when they were sure that no one was looking.

Because of her Dad's job, Sybil had developed an interest in governmental affairs. While she hadn't declared a major as yet, Sybil was seriously considering foreign service for her major. Moshe found out that he enjoyed working with plants and agriculture. His class in biology was one of his favorites, and he was convinced that he would declare either agriculture or biology as his major.

Sybil loved it when Moshe would show up at her job to surprise her.

Her daydreaming time came to an end. The bus was just coming to Sybil's stop. Clearly, Sybil worried. What had happened? Was Moshe all right? When Sybil got to the bookstore, she saw her friend Ruthie, who worked the evening shift.

Ruthie was surprised to see Sybil at the store. She wasn't on the schedule for today. "Well hi, stranger. What are you doing here on your night off." Sybil didn't answer. "Looking to buy a book?"

Sybil smiled. "I'm meeting Moshe here," Sybil replied in an insistent kind of tone. Ruthie smiled back and started to walk towards the storeroom In the back of the store. Sybil thought about Moshe, who was on his way over, and knew that she needed a chance to talk with him alone.

She walked quickly to catch Ruthie. "Ruthie," she said, "I need your key to the secure store room." Ruthie knew Sybil as a friend and could tell that whatever happened was pretty important. "Sure, Syb. Here's my key. Say hello for me," she said, as she gave Sybil the key and headed off to a different part of the store.

Not many customers were coming in or leaving. It was dinner time as well as the Sabbath, so things were quiet. Sybil stood near the front entrance, waiting. All kinds of thoughts were running through her head until she saw Moshe walking from the bus. He looked terrible, she thought. He obviously had been crying.

When Moshe came into the store, Sybil ran over to him and said, "Oh Moshe, you've had me so worried. Are you all right?" He didn't smile, but just gave her a look.

"Where can we go to talk?" Moshe asked.

"Ruthie lent me her key to the secure storeroom. We can go there to talk." Sybil knew that there was a special room near the general supply storeroom where items that needed to be locked could be secured. He nodded, but didn't say much. He seemed so distracted, she thought. Once they were inside the secure store room, Moshe sat down in one of the chairs. Sybil sat down next to him. "What's wrong, Moshie? she asked him. "What's happened?"

He stopped and looked at her for a moment, more seriously than he ever did before. "Look, Sybil, I have something I have to tell you. I hope you won't hate me for not telling you this before." Sybil nodded and waited for him to go on. He said, "Remember when I told you that my brother Benjamin worked in the fields?"

"Yes."

"Well, it's only partly true. You see, he does work in the fields, but what I didn't tell you is that he's a member of the Resistance."

She seemed puzzled as she repeated the word "Resistance." She asked him, "What does that mean?"

"It's a group of guys he belongs to. He goes there every week."

"I get that part about the weekly meeting, but what for?"

"Benjy tells me that they talk about the land, about the Brits, about the Arabs, and stuff like that. All I've heard is that there's always a lot of talk."

"What's wrong with talk?"

"Talking about hoping to change things. That's all I heard from Benjy until today. But now he's arrested. And now I've learned more."

"Arrested?" Sybil asked. "How? Why?"

"I called his friend, Hirschl. And I found out. Benjy had a gun today; Hirshl loaned it to him."

"But why, Moshe? Why did he need a gun?" Sybil asked.

"It seems that Benjy was going with one idea in his head. To start things up. He thought if he went to the Fort at Acre and shot a gun off, it would send a message to the Brits."

All Sybil could say was "Wow."

"Now what?" she asked him.

"And now he's in prison. Just like my Papa was."

Sybil looked at Moshe. He looked like he was on the verge of tears.

"I've always looked up to him. I always felt that Benjy seemed to know how to handle himself, always trying to do the right thing," he added. Sybil looked at him. His face was a mask of sadness. He started to choke up, and then he cried. And then he was sobbing.

Sybil put her arms around him and hugged him and softly said, "Oh, Moshie." In this moment Sybil felt so incredibly moved and close to him.

Moshe stopped his crying and looked at her. "I didn't know who else to turn to, Syb," Moshe said.

"Oh Moshie, I love you so." They kissed and hugged. "You know I'll be here for you, Moshie. Don't worry, we'll get through this."

Sybil gave Moshe an even more tender and sweeter kiss. A kiss so very warm and passionate that she could feel her heart racing. Sybil knew what she wanted to do. "There's something I need to do," she said to Moshe. "Stay here. I'll be right back."

There was a small bathroom in the secure storage area. Sybil walked over to the bathroom and closed the door behind her. Her heart was beating so fast as she thought about what she wanted to do. Sybil looked at her face in the mirror. She knew that if she went ahead with it that it would be so unexpected that it would certainly cheer Moshe up. Sybil decided to go ahead with it. Oh, she had let one or two boys touch her leg under her dress once or twice before, but this was certainly going further with a boy than she had ever gone. Sybil was so nervous as she opened the buttons on her blouse that her hands were shaking. She took off her blouse, removed her bra, and stuffed it in her bag. Sybil put her blouse back on but didn't button it. She then got up and, holding her blouse closed, came back into the room where Moshe was sitting. She sat down next to Moshe and leaned into him as she said, "I've never gone this far with a boy before, Moshe, but I knew I wanted to with you."

Sybil let the blouse fall open. Moshe's eyes widened and he couldn't stop looking. He reached out his hand and tried to stop shaking from excitement and nervousness as he touched her breast. Sybil let out a little moan as she let him touch her. Moshe wrapped his arms around Sybil and kissed her so passionately. They just held each other for a few minutes, not saying anything. Sybil felt a tingly feeling and moaned as his hand gently circled her breast and then the other one. Moshe wanted to go further as his hands went toward her dress. "Please let me, please let me," he said. A warmth of desire spread across Sybil's body as she decided to let him undress her.

Slowly, with shaking hands, Moshe took Sybil's blouse off, reached down and tried to pull off her skirt, but he didn't know where the snap on the side of the skirt was located. Sybil reached around and unsnapped it and stepped out of it. Moshe reached over and gently pulled Sybil's panties off. Sybil was totally nude. She was shivering from a combination of nerves and excitement. Also, the secure store room seemed to be kept at a lower temperature. Moshe hugged Sybil, then told her to lay back and bring her knees up until they touched her chest. Sybil let out low moans as Moshe pushed himself on her and tried to enter her. "Ow, ow," she cried. He tried again. "Ow. Ow. Moshie, stop. Stop. You're hurting me," she yelled.

She looked down at her pelvis and saw blood. She started to cry and reached for her clothes now lying in a heap on the floor. She felt very stupid and very alone. As Sybil started putting her clothes back on, Moshe just sat there looking at her. "I'm sorry, Sybil," Moshe started to say. Just then there was a knock on the door.

It was Ruthie.

"I need to get in here, Syb," she said as both Moshe and Sybil were scrambling to put their clothes back on.

"Give me a few minutes, Ruthie. OK?" Sybil said.

"OK, I'll be right back."

Moshe and Sybil had barely finished when there was a knock on the door and Sybil let Ruthie in. "I'm sorry, you two, but I needed to get some supplies from the secure storage area. Just ignore me and I'll be out of your way in a moment," Ruthie said. They just sat there until Ruthie had left.

Moshe said something first. "I'm sorry, Sybil, I really am. I didn't mean to hurt you."

"I know," Sybil responded. She stopped and looked at Moshe. She really felt bad about what happened. "Look, Moshe, I know you feel bad. I feel bad, too. I wanted this as much as you," Sybil said. Moshe went over to try to give Sybil a hug but she stopped him, saying, "Just take me home, Moshe. I want to get home." There was a plea in her voice— and she sounded not like a woman, but more like a scared little girl. Moshe helped Sybil collect her things and they both left the store room. He gently kissed Sybil on the cheek and she smiled back. "I do love you, you know," she said to Moshe.

"I know," he replied.

Moshe walked Sybil over to the bus stop and waited until the bus came. When the bus arrived, Moshe helped Sybil get on, and on an impulse, he got on, paid the fare for both of them and stayed on the bus with Sybil. As she rode home, she snuggled up with Moshe seated next to her. Sybil thought about the day....about Moshe.... What had happened in the storeroom was not how Sybil pictured it would be but, in a way, she was glad that they had taken their love to a new place.

And she meant it when she told Moshe that she would be there for him.

So many uncertainties, especially now that Benjamin was in jail, she thought. Now Moshe would have to take on more responsibility around the house and be there for his mother and sister. And then there was another equally important matter looming up ahead. How and when should Sybil tell her Mum and Dad that she was in love with a Jewish boy? Could they look past his religion to see what a great guy he was and how happy Sybil had been since they met. Where would they be in six months? Sybil couldn't be sure and Moshe certainly didn't know.

She was glad that she had her parents had a home and a warm bed waiting. Sybil and Moshe both agreed that it would be best to take off a few days from seeing each other. When they next saw each other at the university library a week later, it was clear that their affection for each other hadn't diminished but actually may have gotten stronger.

Sybil waited anxiously for Wednesday, 10 May, to arrive. She knew that her parents were going to Haifa for a meeting, conference and reception that would keep them out until late at night. Once she knew that her parents were on their way, it was Sybil's plan to show Moshe her parent's apartment, especially her room. That night, by 6 pm, Moshe had arrived by bus and they grabbed a bite at the nearby Middle Eastern cafe. Sybil dialed her phone and let it ring enough times to be sure that her folks weren't home. Then she brought Moshe to the apartment. He said he really liked it, especially her room. When Sybil brought Moshe into her bedroom she said, "I was such a ninny for the way I behaved last week, Moshe. I love you, you know."

"I know."

"I want you to take me to bed, Moshe," Sybil said. Then they both undressed and made love under the covers in Sybil's bedroom.

It was wonderful.

Afterwards they cleaned up, straightened up the bedroom, and then shared more kisses on the street outside the apartment, before Moshe headed back home.

Chapter 4

It was so cold during the night that Benjamin's teeth were chattering. The thin blanket on the cot barely covered him. In his mind's eye he relived the events of a month ago all over again—getting a lift to Rose Pinah, firing the gun, being forced to the ground, handcuffed, questioned. It seemed like a long time had passed before two soldiers brought him to the cell. He figured he was in the Acre prison, even though no one had come to talk to him since then. The only view was of the thick black cell door.

Sleep had been almost impossible. He could hear the others–loud talking, screams, mixed in with some curses in Hebrew and cursing in Arabic. In the middle of the night the prisoner in a cell nearby tried to talk with him. At least that's who he thought it was. But he was afraid to say anything—it could be a trap, he figured.

The sun came up, that much he was able to tell from a glint of it reflecting on a window that must be down the hall. He looked around the cell. There was dirt and grease on every surface. Benjamin stared at the sink with its one working faucet that spewed cold water, at the toilet where there was no seat to lift up—just an opening where the waste went down. Like everything else in the cell, it hadn't been cleaned in a long time. The place reeked from the smell of disinfectant mixed with the odors of urine and body odor.

After twenty four hours he actually got used to it.

It was quiet in the morning but that soon changed.

He was sitting on the cot looking at the scratches on the wall and mentally adding them up when he noticed a British soldier—a Private, he figured. The private was walking slowly down the row of cells, stopping at each one to wordlessly stare. He had a clipboard and he looked at it and at each prisoner and marked something down. As he walked he frequently reached for the grip of the gun. Not for any reason as far as anyone could tell. Benjamin tried to keep from looking at him directly, figuring it was better not to call attention to himself. Soon, however, the private was standing at his cell door.

"Prisoner!" he shouted, "turn and face me." Benjamin did as he was told. Private Herman Buxton was standing there, glaring. "What's your name?" he shouted. "Yosef," he replied. "Benjamin Yosef." Private Buxton muttered something under his breath, marked something on his clipboard and moved on.

A little late two guards rolled a cart down the row of cells with, what he assumed, was a meal. Gruel, not hot but more like room temperature, was ladled out into a bowl and a roll of hard, crusty bread was placed on top of the gruel. A bent spoon was the only utensil provided, and it was all shoved into an opening at the bottom of the cell by the guard. Benjamin ate ravenously.

It seemed like hours before Benjamin saw anyone other

than the Private. Eventually he dozed off again from sheer boredom but then a voice barked out, "Yosef, you have a visitor." He looked and saw Itzhak Gamel standing there. Buxton opened the cell door for Itzhak, glared at both of them as he said, "Twenty minutes. That's all the time you're allowed." And then he said to Benjamin, "Don't try to escape, prisoner. I will shoot you if you try." He quickly closed the cell door, locked it, turned and left.

Benjamin was so happy to see Itzhak that he threw his arms around him in an embrace. Itzhak smiled back. "How have they treated you?" Itzhak asked.

"All right," Benjamin said. "All things considered, I guess I'm alright."

Itzhak looked at him for a moment, then he continued, "I've heard only bits and pieces of what happened from some of the Brits. I want to hear it from you. I have to say that judging by the way they spoke, I expected to see you bound and whipped by now."

Benjamin said, "These soldiers—they hate me. They've called me a terrorist and a conspirator…"

As they sat talking, Private Buxton deliberately walked back and forth in front of the cell. Itzhak noticed it, and in a soft voice said, "Easy, Ben…. Don't say any more than you have to. Especially in front of that private. He's acting like he could easily pull the trigger for no reason." They stopped talking until Buxton left.

Once he left, Itzhak continued, "What did happen on the Rose Pinah Highway? Tell me… and don't leave out any details, no matter how insignificant they might seem to be," he said. "I'm going to sit in this chair and give you my undivided attention."

Benjamin started, haltingly at first, but Itzhak sat there,

not saying a word, giving him a smile and a nod of understanding.

Benjamin explained, "Well, it was about 3:00 in the afternoon. I was walking on the road from Safed to Rose Pinah."

"Were you alone?" Itzhak asked. He leaned forward in the chair, paying even more attention as Benjamin answered.

"A truck carrying some vegetables passed by as I walked," Benjamin explained. "Then I saw a truck with a canvas top pass by. I don't know why I did it. But it was like I was angry or something... I lifted my pistol up into the air—straight up, like this, and fired one shot." Benjamin stopped and looked at Itzhak. He could tell by Itzhak's expression that he was impatient, wanting to know more.

Itzhak asked, "Did you know what kind of a truck it was?"

"No, I didn't," Benjamin replied.

"And then what happened, Ben?"

"The truck stopped and all of a sudden there was a bunch of soldiers," Benjamin then continued, "Brits jumped out from the back. They surrounded me. They were pointing their rifles at me. I dropped my pistol. They forced me to the ground—laying on my face. They put me in the back of the truck and took me here."

Itzhak stopped and looked at Benjamin for a moment, as if in disbelief. Then he reached inside his suit jacket pocket and pulled out a clean piece of paper. He then folded the paper in half and wrote at the top of the page. Benjamin couldn't see what Itzhak was writing but it must have been a brief thought or two. Then Itzhak folded the paper and put it in the inside pocket of his jacket. "Did anybody pass by?" Itzhak asked.

Benjamin shook his head and said, "No. Not when I shot the bullet."

Itzhak continued, "So there were no witnesses?" "No, Not any that I saw," Benjamin replied.

Itzhak stood up for a moment. Whether to stretch his legs or for some other reason, but Benjamin couldn't tell why. Suddenly, Itzhak wheeled around and said "All right. Let's go over this again. You're standing on the side of a road. You see a truck and shoot a bullet into the air? Why?" He stopped, folded his arms and stood quietly waiting for Benjamin's reply.

"Why?" Benjamin asked rhetorically. "It just happened, that's all," he added.

Itzhak looked at him for a moment and then reached for his coat. "Ben......" He paused, shook his head, and added "I'm gonna have to be going, now." They both knew right away that Itzhak wasn't buying it.

"Huh? Going?" Benjamin asked. "But aren't you going to help me defend myself?"

Itzhak walked a few feet to the locked cell door, turned and said, "I can't help you until you start telling me the truth. Now come on, you and I both know you've been making up a story....So either you tell me what really happened or I'm on the next bus back to the city....." They just stood there for a few moments looking at each other, getting ready for an argument. But Benjamin was tired...tired of the fear, tired of the loneliness, not knowing what was going to happen next and so it all came out..all of it....

Benjamin talked quickly and non-stop... "All right....all right......I wanted to take some action. I wanted things to happen...to let them know that we weren't going to sit by while they occupied our land," he said.

Itzhak screamed at him, "You knew that the truck you shot at belonged to the British Army. Didn't you?"

Benjamin froze.

Itzhak asked again, even louder and more deliberately, "Didn't you? Talk to me, Ben. Tell me," he said.

"You're right....you're right," Benjamin answered. "I did know. It had markings on the side. I knew right away it was military."

Itzhak sat down in the chair. He seemed drained. He spoke in measured tones, slowly but forcefully, "Didn't anything that I said at the warehouse last week mean anything to you?" he asked. "Do you realize what you've done?"

"I don't want to talk about it any more," Benjamin replied.

"You never did stop to consider the consequences before you acted," he added.

"I don't give a damn. There, I said it," Benjamin said.

There was nothing more to say at the moment.

At least that's what Benjamin thought. He knew the visit was over and expected the guard to come in at any moment.

But Itzhak had something more that he wanted to say. He took a couple of steps toward Benjamin, leaned into him and in a voice barely above a whisper said, "Don't underestimate them. The Brits can see to it that you spend the rest of your life within these four walls. I'm just hoping that we can get you off with a light sentence. Well, at least I have something I can use to begin a defense."

Just as he said it, the guard was at the cell door, opened it, and let Itzhak out.

"I'll be back in a day or so, Ben," he said, and he was gone.

The days and nights dragged by after that jail cell meeting.

Whatever sleep Benjamin was able to get came in fits and starts. He could hear the screams of the prisoners, could smell the fetid air of the prison mixed in with strong, very strong disinfectant. He tried to remember different events and people in his life, but couldn't focus. Increasingly he felt tired and weak, like he had a flu. He figured he had a temperature, but no one was paying attention to him except to push a tray of food under his cell door and take a head count in the morning and the evening. It would be several weeks before he would see Itzhak again.

Chapter 5

It was early afternoon in the Hargrove home. Sybil's mother, Millicent, was ironing her husband's shirts. Ted, her husband, was busy at the home office. Classes at the university were done for the day.

Which left plenty of time for Sybil to worry. What to say to Mum and Dad? How to tell them that she met the "boy"… the man of her dreams.

Sybil had wrestled with her feelings these last two weeks since she and Moshe had their first true intimate moment in the back of the bookstore. Granted, it hadn't been all she hoped it would be, but their lovemaking in her bedroom confirmed her feeling that Moshe was the man she wanted in her life always.

Ever since their last date she had not heard from Moshe and started to worry that maybe he didn't really love her. Maybe he was just using her. Or worse, maybe he thought she was too "easy." And then a letter came addressed to her without a return address. Sybil waited until she was alone to read it. She knew it had to be from Moshe.

"My dear sweet beautiful Syb," he wrote. "How beautiful our last date was. I'm sorry that we haven't been together since then. I have been so busy looking after my mother. She has been so downhearted since Benjy's arrest that all she does is sit and cry. Please know that I love you with all my heart and want to see you soon. And tell you in person. All my love, your Moshe."

As she read the note, tears came to her eyes and she could feel her heart beating faster. She dreamed about him. His face...his hands...his back....the freckles on his arms... she knew she was a "silly nit" but she couldn't help it, she loved him. It seemed like the best time to bring the matter up was when Mum would be preparing breakfast and serving it to Dad. He was always in a rush to get to the office. So bright and early the next morning Sybil came into the dining room.

Her Mum had already served her Dad his breakfast and, true to form, he already had his nose buried in the paper while he ate his toast and jam and drank his tea. "Morning Mum, morning Dad," Sybil said as she sat down at the table across from her Dad. "You're up early today, Syb," her Mum noted. "Do you want some toast with jam, like Dad's having?" she asked.

"Yes, Mum, that would be great," Sybil responded.

As Millie toasted the bread, boiled the water in the kettle for the tea and spread the jam for the toast, she said, "A letter came for you yesterday without any return address."

Sybil answered quickly, "Yes, Mum. It was for me. From a friend in school."

Sybil's dad, Ted, peered at her over his paper. "A friend you see every day at school writes you notes?" he asked. "Must be a boy."

"Yes, Dad," Sybil said. "But he's a man."

Ted muttered to himself as he silently chewed his toast.

Sybil sat down at the table across from her Dad and started to eat, nervously. She had a textbook from school that she buried her head in, waiting for the questions from her father. She glanced over at her father who had picked up the paper, found where he left off, and resumed his reading. As he read he continued eating, all the time muttering to himself.

Millie joined them at the table and, as she stirred her tea, she asked Sybil "How did you meet him?" Sybil quickly volunteered that "he goes to the same school that I do. He came into the bookstore and we kind of hit it off," she answered.

"Sounds good. What's his name?" Ted asked.

Sybil buried her head into the book and said, "Dad, can I finish reading this chapter? It's for school."

Ted replied "Sure, dear." And then he stopped eating, lowered his paper and asked, "Is there a reason why you're not telling me his name?"

Sybil averted his stare, more of a glare really. He could be so intense sometimes, she thought, as she said, "No, not really, Dad. It's just that I have to get this reading done."

Ted was about to say something more when Millie intervened. "Ted, don't pick on her. I'm sure everything is fine. He's a university student. And the important thing is that Sybil likes him."

Ted looked a little forlorn as he folded his newspaper in half, got up from the table, went over to the coat closet and got his briefcase, placed the paper in it, and closed the latch. He put on his coat and hat and took one last look in the mirror in the inside of the closet. As he started to go to the door he turned to Sybil and said, "Well, young lady, you're off the hook for now. But I want to hear more about your young man when I come home this evening."

Both Sybil and Millie went over to Ted and gave him a kiss.

Millie said "Have a good day, dear," and they watched Ted go. Then Millie turned to Sybil and said, "All right, Syb. Tell me about him."

Sybil gave her mother a look and was so close to tears... the words came spilling out, "Mummy, I need your help. I met a boy. I fell in love. It happened so quickly. I love him so much," she said.

Millie held Sybil and could feel her body shake with emotion. "Honey, it's all right," Millie said. "Now what aren't you telling me?" There was a definite pause...Millie waited for Sybil to reply. "Are you in some kind of trouble?"

Sybil answered "No, Mum."

Sybil knew it was coming...that look of disapproval and concern at the same time that her Mum would give her once in a while. What could she do? Especially when Millie got up from her chair and sat across from Sybil and, in a quiet voice, said, "Then what is it....I know you well enough to know when something's bothering you. And whether you're going to tell me now...or when you're ready....I'm ready to hear it." Millie knew she had put it out there—she knew her Syb. She felt so close to her daughter that if there were any secrets that Sybil was holding back, she would share them pretty quickly.

And with her next breath, Sybil blurted it right out, "All right, all right. I'll tell you."

"Go on, Millie," said.

Sybil responded. "His name is Moshe. He's a Jewish boy. He's in university but he's not in any of the same classes that I have. He came into the bookstore. We talked—for hours. He seemed so sweet, so kind."

Rather nervously, Millie added, "Go on."

"Well, you and Dad always said you will know when the right guy comes along….And I have," Sybil said.

"Your Dad will be upset."

"I know, Mum."

"Do you really love him? Or is this one of your infatuations?"

"I really, really love him," Sybil said. "We've talked forever it seems…about our hopes, our dreams." Millie knew how overprotective Ted was when it came to his daughter. Hearing about a boy, especially one who wasn't of the same religion…

Millie got up from the table rather quickly, Sybil noticed. She went straight to the kitchen, picked up a sponge and started scrubbing the kitchen sink. And as she scrubbed Millie said, "Your Dad is going to be very angry when he finds out. He was afraid that with us living here you wouldn't meet boys more suited to…" Millie stopped in mid-sentence. She knew what she wanted to say but thought better of it.

"What, Mum? Say it," Sybil said. "I wouldn't meet nice British boys. Catholics or Anglicans. You can say it, Mum," she added.

"You're backing me up into a corner," Millie said.

And then Sybil, usually quiet and reserved, said what was on both of their minds, "Say it, Mum. I've fallen in love. With a Jew."

Millie said, "You know you're putting your Mum and Dad in a difficult position."

Sybil said, "Look, I know it's going to sound terrible but I can't worry about it. I've got to do what I feel. I hope you understand, Mum."

"I'm trying, Syb. I really am."

Sybil got up out of her chair and went into the kitchen and poured some more tea from the kettle. Millie sat very still, quietly taking in all of this argument. When Sybil came back into the room, it was clear that Millie was crying. Millie said, "You have upset me very much, Sybil."

"I know, Mum," Sybil said. She stood up and walked over to the chair where Millie was sitting.

She tried to reach out her hand to stroke her mother's arm but, surprisingly, Millie pulled away and said, "You know it's your Dad you're going to have to deal with." Millie stood up and started to walk towards the kitchen. She was always such a stickler for a clean home. But now with all this upset she hadn't even thought about the dining room table and the dirty china at every place setting.

As Millie walked towards the kitchen, Sybil followed her. She was almost directly behind her mother when she asked, "Will you back me up, Mummy?

Millie quickly turned around so that she was looking directly at her daughter as she said, "It's hard. It's really hard. You're asking me to go against your father."

Sybil asked her, "Well, will you?"

"I'm going to have to wait and see, Syb," Millie said. "That's all I can say.....So we'll have to let it go at that and wait til your Dad gets home later," Millie added, as she left and went into the bathroom.

The tension of the afternoon left Millie weeping. In her bedroom, Sybil was weeping on her pillow. It would be a long day until Ted would be coming home.

The hour hand on the grandfather clock in the living room seemed to tick slower than Sybil had ever remembered. Eventually it was six o'clock and dinner. Apprehensively, Sybil came into the dining room and sat in her usual spot at the table. She made sure to have a book with her and to be busy in it before her Dad's key was in the lock. Millie greeted Ted in the living room. He washed up, changed into his dressing robe and sat, as he always did, at the head of the table.

After the usual "How was your day?" and "What's new?" he turned his attention to Sybil. She tried to avert her eyes and, while she was looking at the pages in the book, she really wasn't aware of what she was reading. It was only a matter of time before Ted said, "Hello, Syb. How was your day?" Sybil exchanged nervous glances with her mother as her father said, "Shall we continue where we left off this morning, Sybil?"

"Oh Dad. Must you start right in?" she replied.

Millie tried to intervene by saying "Ted, eat something first."

But Ted waved her away, saying, "Start right in? Am I starting right in, Sybil?

"Whatever you think, Dad," Sybil answered.

Ted replied, "No, it's not whatever I think, young lady. This morning I found you so elusive, so evasive. You're seeing someone…. a university student. That much we gathered."

Sybil said "Yes Dad, I know."

"Who is he? Where did you meet him? What's his family background? You know I'm tenacious at the office about these details," he said.

Sybil quickly answered back with "I know you are, Dad. But we're not in your office now." She got up from the table, started to walk towards the kitchen, but then she stopped. She thought, why not let her father know who she's seeing and how she feels?

Ted's eyes opened wide as Sybil said, "All right, Dad. I'll tell you about my friend. His name is Moshe Yosef. He's a freshman at the University. He came into the bookstore and we hit it off."

"He's a Jew?" Ted asked.

Sybil quickly responded, "Yes, Dad. He's a Jew….Can you look past that? I love him. He makes me happy. I believe in his dreams, his ideals."

Ted asked, "Dreams? What dreams?"

Millie tried to intervene, but Ted waved her away.

Sybil, though, was ready for an argument. She asked Ted, "Is that all you care about? That he's a Jew? Can't you see past that? Can't you understand? I love him."

Ted was ready for an argument, too. He answered, "What do you want me to say? …You don't know what love is."

Sybil answered back with, "I do know. He's not the first boy I've known…"

That's when Millie, usually so quiet, so patient, jumped up and got between the two of them and said, "Sybil! Ted! Now I want everyone to calm down….Ted…sit down…right here. Syb. Sit down. Over here…Now we're going to get this all out on the table. Let's talk to each other. Instead of yelling at each other. There was an awkward pause while Sybil and Ted sat down across from each other, eyeing the other warily.

Then Ted broke the silence and said "You're right, Millie. We need to keep this civilized."

Millie said, "Yes, we do. Even if I have to stand here between the two of you. She continued, "Now look, Sybil. I understand you love this boy. But your Dad's right—we don't know anything about him."

Sybil said, "He's a nice boy. He's very polite. Very quiet. He's a student. We've had many talks, many conversations."

"About what?" Ted asked.

Sybil quickly jumped up, saying, "No, no. It's private. I'm not going to tell you. I don't have to…"

" As long as you're living in my house, you're going to….." Ted answered.

Sybil ran out of the room, yelling and in tears, saying "I can't talk to you. I can't."

Millie called after her, "Syb! Come back here, Syb!"

They heard her slam her bedroom door and could hear Sybil weeping. Ted stood there, looking at Millie, and said, "Well, what do you want me to say?"

Millie said, "You didn't handle that very well…"

"No, I guess I didn't," Ted replied.

Milie said, "I'll go and talk with her. You don't realize how serious she is…She really loves him. I don't want to lose her."

"Lose her? What do you mean?" But by this point Millie went to Sybil's door, knocked on it softly, but her daughter wouldn't answer.

Sybil knew that she had to go. She waited until her parents had gone to bed. She packed some things in a duffle bag and quietly left to be with her Moshe.

Chapter 6

It seemed like it was going to be another long and tiring day for Itzhak Gamel.

Most knew him from Shul or from his work as an attorney practicing general law in a small, book-lined office on Ben Yehuda Street in Jerusalem. Few knew that he was the legal counsel to the Resistance for the Ben Yehuda cell, and until they could properly fill their ranks with young men and women passionate enough, properly trained and armed, he was satisfied to leave it at that.

Main thing on his calendar today was to see Benjamin Yosef at the Fortress of Acre.

It had been a month since Yosef was captured and imprisoned. As he was escorted to Yosef's cell, Itzhak couldn't help but notice the crumbling plaster on the floors, the noise and the stench that almost caused him to gag.

Benjamin seemed happy to see him, but Itzhak noticed the telltale changes of captivity—Ben's face had more of a pallor and his lack of exercise and poor diet showed in the weight he had lost. As he shook Benjamin's hand, Itzhak was reminded of something he had noticed in jail visits before—that the British didn't do more than feed the prisoner a very meager meal, give him a lonely environment, and let him meet with his counsel as infrequently as possible.

The meeting with Benjamin went as well as could be expected, Itzhak thought. After he answered Benjamin's questions about his family, especially reassuring him that his mother was coping with the situation as best she could, Itzhak got down to the main issue—Benjamin's charges and trial. "There really hasn't been any further developments since we asked about your case three weeks ago," Itzhak noted. "The Brits have said that the indictment is under review by the office of the High Commissioner, but they haven't come forth with any additional information."

"So what do we do, Itzhak?"

"I know it's been hard for you, Ben, but there's nothing we can do but wait for them to respond to our formal second request. I'll prepare it this afternoon as soon as I leave." Benjamin nodded. He knew what it meant. More days and weeks of sitting, waiting.

A moment or two later a guard, Private Buxton, came in followed by a British officer. Almost wordlessly, the officer motioned for the private to use his key to open the heavy cell door. The private went into the cell, told Benjamin to turn around and placed cuffs on his wrists. He searched Benjamin quickly to ensure that contraband didn't find its way in. Itzhak didn't have time to say a "shalom" to Benjamin before the lieutenant said to him, "Counselor, please step this way."

Itzhak followed the lieutenant to an alcove, where he assumed he would be asked to show his identification and searched as he was on the way into the facility. Instead, the lieutenant passed a folded note to Itzhak. The note said, "My name is David Bruner. I must see you. It's extremely important. I know who you are, and about your role in the Resistance. Please meet me one week from now at 8:00 pm at the seashore in Tel Aviv at number 5 Ge'ula Street. Please come alone. Will you meet me? If so, please look up and shake your head "yes."

Itzhak looked up and nodded "yes." In the next moment Bruner took the note from Itzhak's hand, nodded to him, and left.

Itzhak tried his best during the week to find out what he could about Lieutenant Bruner, but there wasn't much in the files that the Resistance had that they could share with him. Even though they had barely spoken, Itzhak felt this was a friend.

It was late at night two days later in the home of Mrs. Sarah Yosef. Rebecca Yosef, Benjamin and Moshe's 14-year-old sister, was sitting in her nightgown and robe on the couch, working on her homework. When her brother Moshe came in, he had a girl with him. He held a protective arm around her shoulder as he said, "Beck, this is my girlfriend, Sybil Hargrove." Syb, this is my sister, Rebecca. You can call her Becca or Beck, like I do, " he added.

Sybil said, "Really nice to meet you, Rebecca. I heard so much about you."

Rebecca got up and walked over to Sybil, shook her hand and smiled as she said, "So you're the friend in the bookstore that Moshie keeps talking about."

Sybil laughed, turned to Moshe, and kiddingly said: "Oh, so you talk about me, huh? Good stuff, I hope."

Rebecca watched as they hugged, and Sybil gave Moshe a kiss. "Syb…not in front of the k-i-d," Moshe said.

"Moshie, I'm not a kid. I'm a woman."

Moshe put his arms around Rebecca in a gentle "bear hug" while saying, "Yeah, yeah. So you are. You're also a pest. Do you know that?" he added as he tried to tickle her. They rough-housed for a few minutes, Rebecca screaming with delight at her brother.

While Moshe and Rebecca were kidding around Sybil was looking around the apartment, especially at the pictures of Benjamin, Moshe, Rebecca and their father in a framed photo. "What a lovely picture," Sybil noted. Moshe stopped and went over to look at the family picture.

"I was a young boy," Moshe said. "I miss my Abba very much," he added.

Sybil gave Moshe a strong hug and then leaned over and whispered in Moshe's ear. Moshe nodded his head, crossed over to where Rebecca was seated and very gently said, "Listen, Beck, we need your help." Rebecca's bright cheery smile dissolved as she looked at the now-serious looking faces that Moshe and Sybil were wearing.

Rebecca asked "What's up?

"You gotta make a promise," Moshe said. "A really important one. Will you promise?"

"I guess so," she said. "Yeah, I guess that will be OK. What do I have to do, Moshie?"

Moshe said, "We're here to get some things and then we have to go." Moshe went into his bedroom and came back with a duffel bag. He quickly crammed some pants, shirts, underwear and socks in the bag.

Rebecca, obviously shocked, asked him, "Go? Where are you going?"

"Listen. I love you," he said. "You're a great kid. You really are. But I can't tell you that."

Rebecca started to cry as she asked, "Are you going for good? Moshie, talk to me. Tell me. Are you going for good?"

Instinctively, Moshe went over and hugged Rebecca as hard as he knew how and said, "Yes, Becca, I am going. Sybil's coming with me." He walked over to Sybil and put his arm around her and said, "Her folks don't understand her. They're giving her a hard time." He added, "We love each other. We're going to be together."

"But what about Mama? You gonna tell her?" Rebecca asked.

"No, Beck. We're not," Moshe replied. "Now look, we gotta go. Now."

Suddenly Sarah's voice could be heard from her bedroom. "Moshe, is that you?" she asked.

"Yes, Mama. I have to go out for a little while. Go to sleep, Mama. Goodnight."

"Goodnight, " she called out.

Moshe, Sybil and Rebecca stood quietly for a few minutes until they were sure that Sarah had gone back to sleep.

Then, once he was sure that there was quiet, Moshe said to Rebecca, "Remember, Becca, you don't know anything…" And then, as if for the final time, he gave Rebecca a hug and a kiss.

Sybil said, "Great to meet you, Becca," and gave her a hug.

"Love ya, Sis," Moshe said. "Listen, after we go, like in the morning, give Mama this note. It will explain everything. Take care of Mama."

Rebecca said, "I will! Oh Moshie!" But they were gone.

In her bedroom Rebecca looked at a copy of the same framed picture that was in the living room. The picture of her father, Benjy, Moshe and her. Now it was just her and Mama.

The next morning started on a typical note. Sarah rose early to make breakfast for Moshe and Rebecca. She called from the kitchen as she usually did, "Moshe! Rebecca! Get up!" Sarah shouted.

"Yes, Mama," Rebecca said, as she entered and sat at the dining room table. She started to eat her toast and jam quietly, looking absent-mindedly at a school book she was to read.

"Moshe! Get up! Moshe!" Sarah yelled, but there was no answer. Sarah went into Moshe's bedroom to get him out of bed. A moment or so later Sarah came into the dining room, asking, "Becca, where is Moshe? His bed looks like he didn't sleep in it. Rebecca kept her head buried in the book and said nothing as she tried to eat her toast. "Rebecca!" Sarah yelled. She didn't reply. "REBECCA!"

"What?" Rebecca answered.

"Where is Moshe?" Sarah asked. Rebecca tried to keep her face buried in her book and gave an unintelligible answer but Sarah had enough. "Becca!" Sarah yelled, and grabbed the book away.

Rebecca was clearly shaken and looked up at her mother. "What, Mama?" Rebecca answered.

"Tell me, where is your brother Moshe?

"I don't know where he went, Mama. And that's the truth."

Sarah said, "Went? Where did he go? Why isn't he home? Come on…out with it…all of it!"

Rebecca responded, "Moshe came here last night after you went to bed, Mama. He had a girl with him."

"A girl? Sarah asked.

"Yes, The one he's been talking about. Her name's Sybil. She talks like a Brit."

Sarah said, "I didn't know about a girl. Moshe never told me anything about it."

"There's something else, Mama. Before they left last night, Moshe gave me this letter and told me to give it to you this morning. He said it would explain everything."

Sarah looked at Rebecca and said, "Read it. Go ahead. Tell me what's happened."

Rebecca started to read the letter to her mother, slowly and quietly.

"Dear Mama, By the time you open and read this letter we are on our way to a new and different life. I met a girl, Mama. Her name is Sybil Hargove. I call her Syb. I met her at the university bookstore where she works. She's a Brit and she's also twenty. Her father is some kind of officer in the High Command Office. That's all I know about her family. While I haven't met him or Syb's mother, I hear they're nice. There's a note that Syb wrote to her parents. She wrote out their phone number and address, too. Please let them know that she's alright and with me. We love each other very much and hope to get married."

Sarah stood up, stunned. She didn't move for a moment, trying to take this all in. Then Sarah said, more to herself than to her daughter, "Married? They're babies. And she's not Jewish." Then she said, "I have to sit down. This is quite a blow." After a few moments Sarah turned to Rebecca and rested her head on her shoulder. She asked Rebecca, "Is there anything else in his note?"

Rebecca said, "Yes, Mama, there is."

"Well, go on...."

"Mama, I've been so torn up about Benjy being in prison," Rebecca read aloud. She continued to read his letter aloud to her mother. "I feel Benjy's passion and his zeal. I talked about it with Sybil. She feels like I do—that maybe there's something we can do. I hope that you and Becca will be strong and take care of each other. And send our love to Benjy. If I can write again, I will. Please know that I love all of you and never wanted to hurt you. Love, Moshe."

Sarah, her head resting on Rebecca's shoulder, wept inconsolably for a long time. Rebecca tried to comfort her mother, but her mother's constant crying wouldn't stop. Eventually though, Sarah went to her room to lie down. "Resistance." It wasn't the first time she heard the word. It seemed to be in all the newspapers and even on the radio. She decided that she would find out more about it.

Chapter 7

The usual paperwork kept Itzhak busy at his office during the week. The plan to meet in Tel Aviv at the shore was an inconvenience, Itzhak thought, that he could have done without. But Bruner's note seemed so heartfelt, so urgent that it demanded attention. The week seemed to go quickly and it was the day of the meeting. He left his office earlier than usual to get to 5 Ge'ula Street. He parked a few blocks away and walked over to Number 5. It was a nondescript building. Around back was a stairway leading down to the beach.

Itzhak looked and saw an old weathered bench with a couple of slats missing. He looked at his watch. It was about 6:15. He walked down the steps and sat down on the bench and looked out at the sea. About ten minutes or so later, a tall, thin man, dressed in dark slacks and a thin windbreaker, strode briskly to the bench. Once there, he waved and said "Hello. No last names, please. I'm David."

Itzhak responded with "Itzhak," and he shook David's hand.

"Thanks for coming. Did you tell anybody that you were coming here to meet me?"

"No, no one. I was extremely careful," Itzhak replied.

David nodded. "Good."

Itzhak said. "Now.... tell me why you wanted to meet me."

David said, "Well, as you must have figured it out already, I am a Jew."

Itzhak quickly replied, "I thought so. But why the intrigue? Why all this mystery?"

"It will help if I tell you more about me," David said.

"Go on."

David explained, "Well, In 1941 my parents were living in Hungary. I came over to Palestine to earn a living."

"How old were you?" Itzhak asked.

David went on to explain, "I wasn't a young man. I was 33. Once I got settled, I had hopes of bringing my folks over to Palestine, but the Nazis invaded Hungary. That was in '40."

"Did you go back for them?" Itzhak asked.

David shook his head and said, "I heard through friends of friends that they were taken away. So there was no reason."

Gently, Itzhak said "Go on...."

"I joined the British Army when they were calling for volunteers. I still hoped to go back and find my family. Somehow I dreamed I would reach them and get them out of the Nazi hell."

Itzhak asked, "How long have you been in the Army?"

"Four years. Four horrid years. I finally got back to my hometown two years ago, but, of course, my dream was just that—a dream. My family wasn't there. I couldn't even find their graves....And when I returned here the gates of the country were closed to Jews. This is not what I expected when I joined the British Army."

Itzhak looked at him with a pensive expression and then asked him, "Tell me, David, what did you expect?"

David said, "I thought that if Jewish youths were to fight in the ranks of the British Army, then, when the war was over, Jews would finally get their independence in their own homeland—a free state."

Itzhak responded by saying, "Tell me, you're a Jew. You know what we face…How did you explain all of this to the Brits?"

David answered, "You see, the Brits know I'm a Jew but they think that I have turned against the Jewish cause and love their cause and their ways now. It's taken me a long time to build up confidences between the others and me. They don't know how I really feel."

Itzhak said, "You've heard of the Resistance. You know what we're trying to do."

David responded, "That's why I wanted to see you. I should be struggling and fighting for the liberation of the country of my ancestors. Men like Benjamin Yosef are to be admired. I've been thinking about that—renouncing my British citizenship. But I've been torn—I didn't know what to do."

Itzhak put his hand on David's shoulder, saying, "I can see you've been giving this a lot of thought.

David smiled and relaxed a bit, saying, "I have.…I've thought about life as it was in Hungary."

Itzhak nodded in agreement, saying, "I couldn't agree more. It sounds to me like you have already made up your mind…"

Just then a siren sounded. David noticeably stiffened and

quietly said to Itzhak, "I'm sure the RMPs are patrolling. When they get here let me do the talking. Just know you have my thanks and gratitude." He added, "I'll be in touch."

It couldn't have been more than ten minutes when a "Red Cap" came marching down the street, saw David and Itzhak talking, and approached them. He said, "I have been authorized by the Commander-in-Chief of the Royal Military Police to stop and search residents for identification and any concealed weapons that they might have. Your identification, please."

David quickly and firmly said, "We are not carrying any weapons, Lieutenant. I give you my word." Itzhak gave his wallet to the lieutenant, who did a cursory examination of his ID and a brief "pat down" and then asked, "You live in Jerusalem, Mr. Gamel. Why so far from home this evening?"

Itzhak handled it cooly, didn't fluster, and in a matter-of-fact voice said, "Just visiting with my old friend, David." Itzhak knew to look at the lieutenant and not do anything that would raise suspicion. The lieutenant quickly returned Itzhak's ID back to him and then looked at David's ID. The lieutenant said, "Your identification says that you are a British Army officer. Name, rank and serial number, please."

"David Bruner. Lieutenant. 1485346 Zed," David replied.

The lieutenant asked, "May I ask you, Lieutenant, why you're out of uniform?"

David also knew to remain calm and as matter-of-fact as possible as he responded, "On twenty-four hour leave today, Lieutenant, visiting with my old friend, Itzhak. It's been a long time since we've seen each other."

David gave Itzhak a warm handshake and they smiled at each other.

The lieutenant carefully "patted down" David and then

returned his ID to him. He saluted David, nodded to Itzhak, said "Thank you, gentlemen. Have a good night." And he strode off.

They waited for a few minutes, looking at the night sky and sea. After they were sure that the lieutenant left, David said, "Look, I'd better be pushing off. I don't want to arouse suspicion."

Itzhak reached inside his suit jacket pocket and gave David his business card, saying, "Call me. Let's talk."

David nodded, went to shake hands, but then, suddenly, he embraced Itzhak. Words weren't needed.

"Goodbye, Itzhak," David said. He felt a wave of emotion and his eyes were moist as he turned and walked down the seashore.

Tears welled up in Itzhak's eyes as he watched David go and softly said, "Goodbye, David. Shalom."

Chapter 8

It's never easy to leave home, Sybil thought to herself as she packed her overnighter. Especially, she thought, when your parents have spoiled you all your life.

Even at her young age, Sybil was worried that she wouldn't meet any suitable young man, let alone someone who would thrill her. But then Moshe came into her life. And in just a matter of a few months, Sybil had gained a boyfriend, lover and best friend.

Her parents were always bringing up one fact to her—that growing up, they didn't have the same advantages that she had.

Her father, Edward Hargove, was born to a London day farmer, Edward Hargrove, Senior, called "Teddy" by friends and family alike, and his wife Frances. Like his father, he was called Teddy when he was a young man, but preferred to be called Ted as he grew older. He had a sister, Joan. Life in London wasn't easy for Teddy and Frances and their two children during the war due to rationing, and was especially horrible during the Blitz aerial bombing attacks on London when the family had to be evacuated to the countryside.

From the time when he was a young boy until he met and married Millie and they moved to their own flat, Ted heard his Dad continually blaming the Jews for all of the evils facing mankind, including Hitler's rise to power. Dinners with Mum, Dad and Millie usually brought out Dad's anger over the Jews and Ted often found himself angry and upset, which didn't help soothe the nervous stomach he developed.

While in London, Ted served as an administrator in His Royal Highness' Foreign Service. His years of devoted and loyal service meant everything to him and Millie. They had a comfortable apartment in London but the opportunity to work in the new post in the British High Command in Palestine was too tempting.

Sybil stuck it out for a while but she knew it was time to leave. She also knew that Moshe felt the same way. So that night, when they left Moshe's mother's home, Sybil called some of her school chums to find a place to stay until the next morning. After several calls it didn't seem promising. But then Ruthie's friend, Devorah called. "Hi Sybil. It's Dev. Ruthie called me and said you need a place to stay tonight," she said.

Sybil said, "Yes, Dev. But it's Moshe and me now. Can we stay with you tonight?" she asked.

Devorah said, "My parents went to Ashkelon to be with my sister. She's due any time now. So you can stay tonight for sure." Sybil wrote the directions to her friend's home down and within a half hour Sybil and Moshe arrived.

Devorah showed them her parent's room and made them promise that they would clean everything up and be out by morning. Then Devorah said good night and went to her room. Sybil and Moshe relished the chance to have the evening alone. They kissed and hugged. Moshe helped Sybil undress and they made love. They fell asleep in each other's arms.

In the morning they hurriedly dressed, made up the bed as they found it, thanked Devorah and headed off for the train station.

For the next few days they rode the trains and buses between Tel Aviv, Jerusalem, Haifa and points to the South. The little money they had was what Sybil was able to take from Millicent's shoe box before she left. After getting through the past few days of travel on buses and trains, Sybil and Moshe felt very weary and discouraged. They catnapped as best they could, but clearly they were both tired and in need of a good meal.

Their plans weren't working out well either. They didn't find the old Rabbi in the old shul near the center of Haifa who would ignore their papers and marry them immediately. Too many questions about who they were, where they came from and where they were headed. Everyone they met seemed too busy to know or care about them. Sybil was worried about her folks. The letter she left them was so abrupt, so unfeeling, that inwardly she agonized about it. "Maybe I should call my Mum and let her know we're all right," she said to Moshe.

"You're with me now, Syb," Moshe said. "They'll be fine," he added. Inwardly, Moshe also agonized over his departure without saying goodbye to his mother. That, combined with the continued worry about his brother Benjy in prison, and his young sister, Rebecca, darkened his usual sunny mood. And added to that was their loneliness—for neither Sybil nor Moshe had ever been away from their families for more than a day or two.

Sybil was homesick for her room, her bed, her school friends. At some points she looked at him and thought to herself "What am I doing here? What do I really know about him, his friends, his life?" There were awkward moments, too, when they didn't have much to say to each other to keep a conversation going. Then Moshe remembered the place that his brother, Benjy, had told him about. "It's an old tobacco warehouse, about a fifteen minute bus ride from the center of town," Moshe said. He told Sybil that his brother and some friends would meet there weekly to talk about current conditions in Palestine, about the Brits, about the Arabs, and they referred to themselves as "the Resistance."

"'Important work' is how Benjy described these meetings," Moshe said. Moshe sat and thought about it, trying to recall details that would help him to locate the place. And then he remembered—"Gamel. I remember the lawyer that's helping Benjy," Moshe said to Sybil. "His name is Itzhak Gamel, and I am pretty sure that his office is in Jerusalem," he added.

Sybil thought it best to find Gamel's office phone number and call as soon as possible.

In half an hour Sybil and Moshe were able to call Itzhak Gamel's law office on Ben Yehuda Street in Jerusalem.

"Yes, Moshe, of course I remember you," Itzhak replied, when Moshe called and identified himself. Itzhak carefully listened as Moshe explained that he and his girlfriend, Sybil, wanted to see him.

"Are either of you in some sort of trouble?" Itzhak asked. Moshe reassured him that they weren't, but would rather talk with him in person. They agreed to come to Itzhak's office in downtown Jerusalem at 15 Ben Yehuda Street.

Since Moshe and Sybil didn't know their way, Itzhak

suggested they board the number 357 bus that would let them off two blocks from his office. It was another hour or so before the buzzer rang in Itzhak's office. He looked through the peephole before buzzing in Moshe and Sybil.

When they came into the outer office Itzhak looked at them. They both looked like they hadn't slept in a month and their clothes looked very rumpled.

After he ushered Sybil and Moshe into his private office, Itzhak shook hands with both of them and smiled. "So tell me where you've been and why you've come to see me," he said. As though a spigot on a faucet had been turned, first Moshe and then Sybil recounted their arduous trip, trying to find a Rabbi to marry them, travelling for three days with meager meals, unsavory restrooms and a lack of companionship. Sybil, especially, seemed very fragile and on edge.

After they told Itzhak about their journey, he knew exactly what to do. He picked up the phone and called his wife Miri, at home. "Miri, I have two young people in my office now. A lovely couple, Moshe and Sybil. They need a place to stay tonight and a hot bath and some of your home cooking," he said. He listened, nodded his head, turned to them and said, "It's settled. You're coming to our home this evening."

They smiled at Itzhak, and Sybil started to cry. Moshe put his arm around her shoulder to comfort her.

"We can't thank you enough, Mr, Gamel," Moshe said. Immediately Sybil and Moshe gloomy looks gave way to smiles.

Sybil and Moshe waited in Itzhak's outer office until 5 o'clock. Moshe gently rubbed Sybil's neck and whispered in her ear. She smiled and laughed at him and teased him back a little. Things didn't seem as hopeless as they had earlier in the day.

They got into Itzhak's car for the short ride to his home. On the way over, besides a little bit of a sightseeing tour of Jerusalem, Itzhak asked Sybil about her family: who they are, what they do for a living. He was careful to keep the questioning light and easy but clearly he was concerned about her father and his role in the High Command. Itzhak made a mental note to find out more about Edward Hargrove as soon as he could.

As soon as they arrived, Miriam came out to greet them. She gave both of them a hug and showed them where they could wash up before prayers and dinner. While Miriam was attending to Moshe and Sybil, Itzhak was calling one of the Resistance members, Chaim, to ask him to find out all he could about Sybil's dad, Edward Hargrove. One thing that Itzhak prided himself on—he took care to be sure that he was always in the know and in control of the situation.

Dinner that night at Itzhak and Miriam Gamel's home was delicious. Miriam cooked chicken and potatoes and a vegetable. Both Sybil and Moshe ate ravenously. After dinner and coffee and cake were finished, Miriam excused herself to wash the dishes. Moshe brought up the question of joining the Resistance movement and waited to hear how Itzhak would react. He didn't have to wait long for a response. "Are you interested in knowing more, perhaps getting involved?" Itzhak asked.

Moshe responded by saying "I am very interested, Itzhak."

Sybil added, "And I am, too."

He looked at them and smiled broadly. "You'll have a good sleep tonight and tomorrow you will come down to a meeting with me. It's late and I have a full calendar tomorrow. My wife will get you settled. Goodnight."

After relaxing in a hot bath, Sybil changed into a nightgown and robe that Miriam brought to her. "My daughter lives in Haifa and has children of her own, so I am lending you one of her nightgowns to wear tonight," Miriam explained.

"Thank you for your kindness, Mrs. Gamel," Sybil said, as she hugged Miriam and kissed her on the cheek.

"I'm Miri," she replied, "and you're more than welcome, I'm sure."

Sybil was asleep within five minutes. Miriam brought Moshe to the guest bedroom, gave him a towel and a pair of her husband's pajamas, and said that he could bathe in the guest bathroom. Then she said goodnight. After a relaxing hot bath, Moshe changed into clean pajamas and settled into bed. Moshe felt relieved that he and Sybil were off "the road" and could get a good sleep. The brief conversation about the Resistance really excited him. It was something to look forward to tomorrow.

As he settled into bed Moshe felt relaxed and was asleep in a few minutes. The voices of Itzhak and Miriam and sounds of breakfast cooking roused Sybil from sleep the next morning. She had never slept more soundly in her life. Nestled under the sheets and a light blanket, she felt more relaxed than she had in more than a week. Moshe was still asleep when there was a knock on the bedroom door, and then on Sybil's bedroom door. Miriam said, "I have breakfast for you. Come down as soon as you're washed and dressed." Within fifteen minutes, Sybil and Moshe were enjoying eggs and toast and jam and hot tea.

Itzhak joined them for a quick coffee, then said, "I

would like to have both of you come with me this evening to our group meeting. I think you will feel right at home. I'll come for you at 6 o'clock. Is that all right?" It was more than all right for Moshe and Sybil. Itzhak went off to work at his office. Miriam said that she had some shopping to do. For the first time in about a week Sybil and Moshe had a chance to sit down and really talk.

"I'm sorry to put you through all of this, Syb," Moshe said.

She gave him a slight smile and sighed. "I'm really a Miss Goody Two-Shoes, Moshe. I really do miss home and my parents."

"I know," Moshe said.

"I've always worried about what my Mum and Dad think. Maybe more than I should."

"I know, Syb."

"I can only imagine how worried they must be now," she said.

Moshe looked at Sybil and at the tears welling up in her eyes. He went over and tried to hug her, but she resisted, saying "No, Moshe. Not now."

Moshe asked, "What do you want to do?"

Sybil thought about it and she knew in her heart what would make her happiest. "Let me call my Mum," she said. "Let me reassure her that I'm OK and we'll go from there."

Moshe agreed. He also told Sybil that he wanted to call his mother and sister and let them know that he was all right, too.

Sybil went over to Moshe and put her arms around him and hugged him. "I do love you, Moshe. Can you forgive me for being such a silly?" she asked. When Miri returned from shopping, Sybil said that she needed to call her mother at home.

If Sybil expected a warm, friendly response from her mother, it wasn't meant to be. Millicent was very angry and upset with her daughter. She said, "Dad and I have been beside ourselves with grief and worry about you."

Sybil said, "I know, Mum."

"Three days ago you left. It's been torture for us. All we got was a phone call from the boy's mother. Three days ago! She said that all she's been doing is crying for her boys."

"I'm so sorry, Mum. I didn't think this out enough," Sybil said. Her mother asked her when she was coming home. Sybil replied, "I know you're angry with me, Mum. But I'm not coming home now. I love Moshe. We're going to be together. I hope you and Dad will learn to accept this."

There was a click on the phone and a dial tone.

Moshe asked Miriam if he could use the phone to call his mother. Rebecca answered the call. "Oh Moshie, are you and Sybil OK?" she asked.

"We're fine, Becca. How are you and Mama doing?"

"I read her your letter, Moshe. She hasn't stopped crying for three days," Rebecca said.

"Well tell her I called to see how you're all doing. Any news on Benjy?"

Rebecca said, "Nothing new, Moshe."

"Listen, Beck, we gotta go. Love ya, Sis. I'll call again."

While Moshe was on the phone with his sister, Sybil ran to the bedroom where she had stayed. Sybil was heartbroken. She felt so very alone. Moshe came into the room. He knew that Sybil was upset. "Look, Syb. It's us now. We have to manage on our own," he said. Sybil knew that Moshe was right. It was time to find their own way.

Chapter 9

S ybil had never held a gun in her life. It was small and a dirty silver color, and as she breathed in its oily smell, she seemed more jittery than she had been before. Along with the other "recruits," as they were called, (two men, David and Danny), Moshe and Sybil had been lined up in the middle of the room facing the wall. Each recruit was given a gun with no bullets. Then, in a step-by-step way, Shlomo, one of the group instructors, patiently and carefully explained how to hold the gun in the right hand while raising the arm straight up until it was at shoulder level, look down the barrel to line up the gun with the target and then squeeze the trigger. Easy enough, she thought when it was first explained to her, but after more than two hours her arm was sore and tired, and she so badly wanted to sit down and rest her eyes for a few minutes. That afternoon, close to a month ago, seemed like a distant memory to Sybil now.

Itzhak decided to take the day and work from home. In the afternoon, he drove Moshe and Sybil to Ben Yehuda Street, parked in the lot behind his office, and walked them over to the meeting place. He gave them a tour of the old tobacco warehouse building, now used for meetings. There was a large front room, and smaller rooms in the back for offices, and a few rooms that were meant for visitors who stayed over. "We're having our regular weekly meeting in about 45 minutes," Itzhak said. "You'll sit in. There are some people I want you to meet," he added.

In the next half hour young men, older men and a woman or two came in, greeted each other, poured some hot water for tea or coffee from the kettle on the stove in the kitchen and went into the front room. Itzhak made it a point to make introductions to Resistance members Ari Weiss, Ellie Stern and Nachum Hecht. "This is Ben Yosef's brother, Moshe, and his friend Sybil," Itzhak said as a way of introduction. Immediately there were handshakes and smiles and words of encouragement.

"How is Benjy doing?" Ellie asked Moshe.

"I guess he's doing alright under the circumstances," Moshe answered. Ellie and his friend Ari nodded their heads in agreement.

Sybil didn't feel quite as comfortable as Moshe did, for most of the men talked to each other and barely noticed her. After a little while, a few men came over to Sybil, nodded their heads, said hello, and sat down in the seats facing the front of the room. Everyone was waiting for the meeting to begin.

It was 7 pm when Itzhak stood up, raised his hand and quieted the group down. "Good evening, my brothers and sisters of the Resistance," Itzhak said. There were cheers to show approval. "We have some new recruits who have joined us. I would like to ask them to stand up. Here we have Daniel Abramowitz, Moshe Yosef, Sybil Hargrove and David

Bruner," he said. The applause filled the hall. Itzhak then asked each recruit to stand up and say something about themselves.

Danny was Nachum Hecht's friend. When he stood up he said "I am glad to be here. I want to do my part to see a free homeland one day," he said. The men sitting around him clapped him on the back, shook his hand and shouted, "Welcome!" The smile on his face stayed the rest of the evening.

It was Moshe's turn next. He stood up but before he could say anything, Itzhak stood up, put his hand on Moshe's shoulder and said, "This is Moshe Yosef. We all know and love his older brother, Benjamin, who sits waiting in a jail cell in Acre Prison, waiting for his trial," Itzhak said. "I want to tell you that I find that same passion in his younger brother, Moshe. We welcome you to our group, Moshe," Itzhak said.

Feeling so incredibly nervous and tongue-tied, "Thank you," was all that Moshe could say before he sat down.

"We haven't seen too many girls who are willing to join our movement," Itzhak noted. He went over to where Sybil was sitting and asked her to stand up. In a way that reminded her of her Dad, Itzhak put his hands on Sybil's shoulders and said, "I want you all to say hello to Sybil Hargrove. Besides being Moshe Yosef's girlfriend, she is also a British citizen. Sybil told me that she wants to stand side-by-side with Moshe and all of us and join our fight for our homeland. I welcome her," he added. The men in the room stood up and clapped their hands vigorously and then sat down.

As she stood there, taking it all in, Sybil's heart was in her throat. "What have I gotten myself into?" she thought to herself.

Itzhak made it a point to silence everybody before he

went on to introduce David. "My brothers and sisters," Itzhak said, "I am honored to introduce David Bruner. He is a Jewish man—a very courageous Jewish man. In order to search for his parents in his native Hungary and take them out of the hands of the Nazis, he had to disguise himself as a turncoat for the British. He lived and worked as a British soldier for several years here in Palestine. Now the truth can be told within these four walls. David Bruner is a Jew. His allegiance is with his fellow Jews in the fight for a truly free homeland for the Jewish people. Join me in welcoming him to our Resistance movement."

Everyone in the room leaped to their feet. The shouts and cheers were overwhelming. It was all too much for David. After all of those years of hiding his true feelings, of being ashamed of himself and of the clothes on his back, to look around at all the people smiling and cheering and calling his name, David bent over, crying deeply.

Sybil was replaying the sight of those clapping people in her mind when Shlomo yelled, "The break is over, recruits." Two hours in the afternoon were spent on map reading—learning what all of the symbols on the map meant and how to plan a route. A lot of time was also spent during the day or, lately, during evening hours, holding planning sessions to talk about the past—discussing which raids and missions worked and why.

Whenever he could, especially lately it seemed, Itzhak would take time out of his law office day to lead these sessions with some of the long-time members of his team. Men like Shlomo, Hirschl and Ari had participated in past actions and proven their value to the Resistance with their courage and willingness to put themselves in dangerous situations. All in the name of the Resistance.

What seemed most interesting, as far as Sybil was concerned, was learning about the history of Palestine and knowing more about the Jewish people.

Moshe especially enjoyed sitting side by side with Sybil, David and Danny when these strategy sessions were going on. Putting aside the fact that Syb was his girlfriend, Moshe felt good about what he was doing, and felt a real connection to these people.

Books from Itzhak's personal library, though dog-eared and yellowing, were found on almost every table or desk in the warehouse. Sybil noted that there were books on a variety of subjects: Torah, European history, philosophy—as well as a copy of "The Odyssey" and even some old *National Geographics*. Even though the books and magazines were old and not in the best condition, it didn't matter. Everyone who came to the meetings seemed so hungry for knowledge—to learn all they could. David, Daniel and Moshe seemed to adjust to the spartan food and the military routine enforced during the indoctrination. In addition to learning to shoot a gun, Shlomo and some of the others had taught them how to drop and roll in case of enemy fire, how to fight in a hand-to-hand combat situation, along with how to respond if captured. Sybil, on the other hand, was finding it very hard to keep up with the men. She seemed breathless most of the time, and really out of shape. She always hated physical education class and ducked out of it as often as she could, so she wasn't terribly surprised that she had little energy by the time the evening came.

It was 6 o'clock and the end of another day at the warehouse. Most of the Resistance fighters who had come earlier in the day either worked or were in school part-time and then headed home for dinner. Just a few had been staying overnight—Sybil, Moshe, Danny and David.

Usually, dinner was the main meal of the day. Fortunately, Shlomo's wife, Dinah, had cooked an extra piece of pot roast on Sunday night and had sent it down with Shlomo on his next trip to the warehouse on Tuesday evening. Sybil made a simple gravy with the drippings from the pan, added in some flour, and some butter and everyone ate heartily. As he did most evenings after dinner, Danny brought out his guitar and played some tunes. No one was paying much attention though.

Moshe turned on the console radio in the front room and he and Sybil listened to Kol Yisroel. He thought it was good for Sybil to listen and learn the Hebrew from the news reporters as they read the stories of the day.

Each of them took a turn on the overnight shift guarding the front door. After nearly six weeks of indoctrination Shlomo announced that the training was done. Later that evening, when they were pretty sure that the others were asleep, Moshe and Sybil snuggled together in a single bed in one of the two backrooms and made love. Afterwards, they talked, openly and honestly.

"I'm afraid, Moshie," Sybil said.

"Of what?" Moshe asked. Of course, he really didn't need to ask. He already knew what had been troubling Sybil ever since their indoctrination started.

"I'm afraid of hurting someone—shooting them or killing them," Sybil answered. "I'm no good at this. Shooting the gun scares me. And I didn't know what I was getting myself into with all of this Resistance business." Sybil began to cry. "I miss my home. I miss my Mum and Dad," she added, weeping.

Moshe tried to comfort her, but Sybil was really upset. She cried and cried until she eventually fell asleep in Moshe's arms. Danny and David had heard Sybil crying, heard Moshe trying to comfort her, and figured that they would leave her and Moshe alone for the rest of the night.

The warm bright sun shining through the window woke Sybil up the next morning. She was alone in the front room. The warehouse seemed especially quiet now that training was over. Sybil got up, washed and dressed. "Where is everybody?" she wondered as she walked from room to room and didn't see a soul. She figured that they must have gone out to shop for food.

Sybil decided that it was a good time to curl up on the couch in the front room with a good book and take advantage of this alone time. But as she sat staring at the magazine that she had in her hand, her mind raced and she pictured her Mum standing in the kitchen, and Dad at the kitchen table reading the paper. All of this reminded Sybil about how blue and lonely she felt. Like every day of the rest of the week, there was little for the recruits to do except read or listen to the radio. They also played cards to pass the time. The general meetings that usually took place in the early evening most days of the week seemed to be shorter and there were only two that were convened.

Something big was brewing, Danny was convinced, and he said so to David, who shrugged his shoulders in response.

Unspoken, but anxiously, they were waiting for something to happen.

It was two days later. 1:30 in the morning. Moshe looked up at David standing at the foot of the bed, shaking him awake.

David was dressed entirely in blackout gear: black shirt,

black pants, black shoes, black socks, and his face and hands were blackened as well. "We move tonight," he said to Moshe. He went into the other room in the back and woke Daniel up and said "It's tonight." Daniel immediately knew what that meant. He was tingling with excitement as he quickly dressed into black shirt, black pants and shoes and applied shoe polish to his hands and face.

Moshe looked at his watch. It couldn't have been more than an hour and half since he and Sybil had fallen asleep in the bed in the back room. Moshe sat up in the bed, reached out and shook Sybil awake. "It's tonight, Syb," he said. Immediately, Sybil knew what that meant. An involuntary chill coursed through her body. As they had practiced numerous times, both Sybil and Moshe quickly dressed in black shirt, pants, black shoes and blackened their hands and faces.

The excitement that David felt thinking about the mission was almost too much to bear. Everyone headed to the main meeting room to grab a quick bite.

It shouldn't have come as a surprise to Sybil, Moshe or Daniel, but it did, as they entered the dimly lit room, to see that the room was filled with Resistance members—some set to go on the mission—already dressed in their black clothes with their faces blackened, while others had come to lend their support and encouragement to this important event. Moshe and Sybil looked around the room. They were surprised to see Itzhak Gamel there. Sybil was going to go over and say "hi" to him but figured that he was probably too busy to notice her.

Shlomo raised his arm above his head and in a voice slightly louder than a whisper, asked everyone in the room to remain silent. It was 3 am. Itzhak walked to the front of the room, climbed up on a chair to address everyone, and said, "My brothers and sisters of the Resistance, may Hashem bless and protect you as you leave on this important mission." Finally, David thought to himself, the time for action had arrived. He looked at his watch—it showed 3:40 am. It was Tuesday, 5 February, 1946, the day that the Ben Yehuda cell of the Jewish Resistance would strike the Supply Fortress at Ramat Gan.

Handshakes and pats on the backs and it was time to go.

Those leaving on the mission got into the two cars parked downstairs and drove towards the fort. It had all been pre-arranged. Yitzy was driving one car and Ezra was driving the other. They waited until they were safely out of downtown before they put their headlights on. At this time of night, with little traffic to deal with, the 48-kilometer trip should take about 50 minutes, Yitzy thought to himself. Hardly anyone in either car spoke as the autos moved quickly along the highway toward their destination.

As part of his scouting run two weeks before, Ezra had checked the area 2 kilometers from the fort's entrance. There he found what looked to be an old unoccupied farmhouse. A small grove of trees behind the main building seemed to be perfect for their staging area. Ezra drew a crude map for reference purposes and tucked it into the inside pouch of his jacket. When he returned to the warehouse that evening two weeks ago, Ezra showed the map to Itzhak, who seemed to be fine with the planned staging site. Now, here they were two weeks later, on their way.

The ride to the staging site was silent—everyone was absorbed in their own thoughts. Once they were almost at the old farmhouse, Ezra and Yitzi turned off their engines and headlights and watched as David, Sybil, Moshe, Daniel and

Hirschl got out of the cars and walked towards the entrance to the fortress. Quietly, stealthily, they moved the 2 kilometers toward the main gate and stopped when they were in visual sight of the sentry post.

Private Horace Ryan and Private George Grayden were standing guard at the sentry post closest to the main entrance of the Fortress. Light banter helped the time go faster. "I tell you, George, that was some goal my nephew kicked," Ryan said.

"Won the game with that one, did he?" Grayden asked.

Suddenly, the sound of a rifle shot pierced the air. A quizzical look crossed Ryan's face as he felt the sharp pain of the bullet as it tore into his gut. He looked down at the growing blood-red stain on the front of his shirt, and silently crumpled to the ground. He was gone in a minute.

Grayden bent over to feel for a pulse but the stare of death told him it was hopeless. He immediately picked up his radio to notify HQ, but didn't get a chance to use it. What he didn't see until it was too late was the rifle now pointing at his temple. "Open the gate and make it quick," Hirschl yelled out. In less than three minutes the gate was opened, Grayden's pistol was confiscated, he was tied up and marched towards the main wing.

Meanwhile, in the main wing of the fort, David Bruner, dressed in the British Army uniform that he had held onto, presented a copy of his military identification to Private Wesley Phelps. Phelps quickly looked over the paperwork and saluted the Lieutenant as he said, "Lieutenant Bruner. I'm Private Phelps. Please state your business here." Bruner knew that he had to stall for a few moments until the others were in place. The sound of a warning shot was the signal he was waiting for. David Bruner held his revolver pointed directly at

Phelps' gut and said, "Put your hands up and don't make a move. We have come in the name of the Resistance to confiscate the arms and ammunition in this fortress. Try to stop us and we'll shoot." He went and seized Phelps' pistol.

At the same time, four other Resistance members, Hirschl Rosenbaum, Daniel Abramowitz, Moshe Yosef and Sybil Hargrove came in. Only Rosenbaum and Abramowitz held rifles. Rosenbaum went out to round up more captives while the others tied up those caught. "And now we'll take the arms. Move!" Bruner barked.

Shortly afterward, Lieutenant Barker and his commanding officer, Captain Rhys Melville, were marched in and ordered to sit down at the point of a rifle. Unbeknownst to Bruner and the others, the two rifle shots that were heard earlier alerted soldiers stationed In the southwest quadrant of the fort that something had happened in the main wing. Four soldiers, their arms drawn, stormed the main wing, firing their pistols. Bruner and Yosef, caught by surprise, were hit. The other Resistance members were quickly captured and their weapons seized. The captured fighters' hands were cuffed behind their backs and they were ordered to sit down on the floor, keeping their legs crossed at the ankles. One of the soldiers stood guard, keeping a pistol pointed at the group.

Captain Melville quickly made two calls—first to the medics so that the wounded could be examined and treated; the second call went to the commanding officer of the fort with a quick summary of the events and current status. Captain Melville walked over to where the guards had placed the wounded men, Bruner and Yosef, lying on the floor, and were watching them until the medics would arrive. It was clear that Bruner had sustained a gunshot wound to his abdomen and that he was writhing in pain.

If Sybil turned her head to the left, from the corner of her eye, she could see where Moshe had been placed. It looked to her like he had been shot in the leg. It was so upsetting to Sybil to see Moshe writhing in pain that she had to turn her head away and try to keep from crying.

Melville ordered that the uninjured captives—Daniel, Hirschl and Sybil—be taken away and locked in a holding cell until they could be processed and questioned. While on the phone, Melville was advised that David Bruner was a Lieutenant in the British Army who had deserted. Captain Melville could see that Bruner's bleeding had been stopped with the aid of a tourniquet. One of the soldiers guarding him lit up a fag for him. Captain Melville asked David, "What's your name?"

"Bruner. My name is David Bruner," he said. "I am a soldier in the Jewish Resistance."

"You fighting for the Jews now, Lieutenant?" Melville asked. Bruner didn't reply but stared straight ahead.

Just then two medics came in, checked Bruner's vital signs, moved him to the stretcher, and transported him away to the infirmary. Melville next went over to talk to Moshe Yosef, now being seen by the medics. "And who are you?" Melville asked.

Through a considerable amount of pain Moshe said, "I'm Moshe Yosef. I'm a student at the University. I'm fighting for the Resistance. We are committed to this cause. To rid this country of you and your protectorate," he added. Melville heard enough. He stepped away and let the medics finish stabilizing Moshe.

Within the hour a kind of calm, but with a heightened sense of security, took over—and everyone resumed their normal duties at the Fort. Within an hour and a half each prisoner was wearing prison garb, fingerprinted, and photographed. Captain Melville knew that the next thing to do would be to interrogate the captured Resistance fighters.

Excruciating ....numbing, burning, searing pain and heat in his belly. David Bruner could vividly recall that moment when the soldier's rifle bullet tore into his gut. Watching his blood spilling from his insides brought him to the edge of nausea. And then he passed out. He was in and out of a drug-induced haze for how long he wasn't sure.

When David finally woke he looked around and knew he was in a ward with other prisoners. It was a brutal place, he thought. It couldn't have been more than a few hours later when two orderlies wordlessly came in with a gurney and body bag, removed the corpse from the bed next to his, and left.

David's movements were limited. He was shackled to the bed so that he couldn't turn over. The thought of looking at his wound made him shudder.

The orderly who came around to each bed in the ward didn't seem to do anything more than empty the bedpans. There was no conversation between the orderly and the patients—just moans and cries of pain that seemed to be constant. David figured it had to be close to a week ago when he was rolled down on a gurney to this ward. Today an Arab-looking older man came into the ward. When he came in, David immediately thought that this must be the doctor. Methodically, with the help of an orderly, and very little conversation, the doctor went to each bed, consulted a record of the patient's name, identification and medical history, examined the patient and wrote notes.

David had mentally counted the beds and figured that there were eight beds on this ward. It had been an hour or more before the doctor had finished examining five patients before he got to David's bed. The doctor's English was flawless. He looked at the chart, said "Bruner" and didn't wait for a confirmation. And David didn't recall hearing the doctor's name when he arrived at David's bed. As the guard watched, the orderly unlocked David's shackles and removed them. He then removed the light blanket so that David could be examined. The doctor didn't say much as he started his examination. For the next fifteen minutes or so, and with the orderly's help, the doctor thoroughly examined both sides of David's body, writing notes as he went along.

Once he reviewed the chart and the x-rays that were stored in the file, he spoke to David, telling him, "You sustained a significant injury, Mr. Bruner. The reports from the field say that you were struck in the abdomen by a .38 caliber shell from a soldier's service revolver. We had to bring you straight away to the operating room." Continuing, the doctor said, "The bullet had ripped open your small intestine and perforated the bowel. We were able to repair them in the operating room. You lost a lot of blood and, of course, you needed a transfusion. Now we have to monitor to be sure that infection doesn't become an issue. I have to tell you that septicemia, or what you might call blood poisoning, is our biggest concern," the doctor added.

David looked at the doctor with a stare—it was too much to absorb all at once. But he knew that he had brought this on himself. There was no one else to blame.

"One more thing I need to tell you, Mr. Bruner," the doctor said. "We had to do a colostomy on a temporary basis to give your colon a chance to heal. The orderly will explain it all to you and help you learn how to manage it."

That was it. The examination was over. The doctor moved

on to other patients. The orderly re-shackled David to the bed and left. For whatever reason, whether fear or sadness or just feeling sorry for himself, tears welled up in David's eyes and he cried softly for awhile. As he cried, he felt a kind of release as he thought, "This is the price you pay for doing what you believe is right."

Chapter 10

A warm sun rose over the Fortress at Ramat Gan.

Sybil had never been in a jail before. The faint smells of urine and vomit mixed in with strong disinfectant seemed to be everywhere. All night long, from the cells around her, she could hear prayers being chanted, mostly in Arabic, screaming and occasional cursing. She tried to sleep, but felt so jumpy and jittery that every noise seemed to startle her awake. There was another woman in the same cell. She was quiet and didn't seem to be speaking any words that Sybil recognized. Occasionally, though, Sybil would hear her murmur under her breath and then cry.

There, in the dimly lit cell, Sybil had the chance to really think about things. She knew she was a good girl. She had never been in trouble before. She always did well in school, had lots of school chums, and adored her Mum and Dad. She also knew that she was in a lot of trouble. She wasn't sure what would happen to her. What if her Dad and Mum found out? The one thing that Sybil knew for sure is that she loves Moshe. He makes her giggle. He's very passionate, she thought. Would they ever be together again? Sybil wasn't sure. "I'll just have to take things as they come," she thought to herself.

From his prior years of experience dealing with these kinds of situations, Captain Rhys Melville knew that he would probably learn more from interrogating the girl. He called downstairs and asked that Sybil Hargrove be prepared and ready for interrogation as soon as possible.

Within the hour Sybil had been brought to the holding area in the bottom of the fort. A female guard conducted a strip search and provided Sybil a fresh prison uniform to wear. The guard brought her to Captain Melville's office. He motioned for the guard to take the handcuffs off. The guard stood in the back of the room.

"Why don't you tell me in your own words who you are and how you got mixed up in all of this?" Melville asked. Haltingly at first, and then rapidly, with more emotion surfacing as she spoke, Sybil gave the basic information—who she is, where she lives, where she attends school. She was asked about her parents—their names and occupations.

"Well my father's name is Edward Hargrove. He's in government. My mother's name is Millicent Hargrove. She's a homemaker, " Sybil said. Melville wrote a note and asked the Guard to deliver it to the guard waiting outside the door. Melville said, "Now, Miss Hargrove. What were you doing with these men? Daniel Abramowitz, Hirschl Rosenbaum, Moshe Yosef, David Bruner." Sybil didn't say anything but stared back.

Melville walked over to where Sybil was seated. He leaned over until his face was so close to hers. "Answers, Miss Hargrove. I want answers. Do you understand?" he screamed at her. Sybil flinched at the yelling. She wasn't used to it. But she knew that the thought of a jail stay or possibly being tortured was worse.

Sybil said, "I'll try to be helpful, but please don't scream at me."

Melville stopped, and in a softer voice he said, "Would you like some water?" Sybil nodded "yes." Melville poured water from the pitcher on the sideboard and waited until Sybil had a chance to drink before he resumed his questioning.

"All right, Miss Hargrove," he said, "we'll take it from the top."

"All right," she replied.

"How do you know Hirschl Rosenbaum?"

"I met him a few weeks ago," she replied.

"Where?"

Sybil said, "At a meeting."

"A meeting? For what purpose?" he asked. As he asked the questions, he raised his voice and leaned forward, waiting for Sybil to respond. But Sybil just sat there. "Miss Hargrove, I need answers to my questions. Do you understand me?" he asked.

"Yes," Sybil said in a quiet voice.

Captain Melville walked over to his desk and waited for a moment. He wasn't letting go. He walked back and sat in a chair opposite to Sybil's and quietly said, "Let's go over this again, Miss Hargrove. What was this meeting about? How did you know about the meeting?" Melville asked. Sybil sat there, appearing distracted or dazed. "Did you go with a friend, or did you come alone?" he added.

Sybil thought for a moment and then quietly said, "I came with a friend. I didn't know what the meeting was about until I got there."

Melville consulted a report on his desk and then asked, "Which friend is that? What's the name of your friend? Is it Hirschl Rosenbaum?"

"No," she replied.

"Is it David Bruner?"

Sybil answered, "No......I just met him the other day."

Melville asked, "It's Moshe Yosef, isn't it?"

"Yes," Sybil replied.

"Is he your friend? Or maybe more than just a friend...."

"Possibly..." Sybil replied.

"Are you intimate with him?" he asked.

Almost instinctively Sybil blushed and said, "I don't have to tell you that."

Melville said, "So he's your boyfriend, is he?"

"Yes."

"Known him for a while?" he asked. She nodded her head.

"How long?"

"A while," she said. "I've lost count."

"Where did you meet him?" Melville asked.

"We met at the bookstore near the University. I'm a student and work there part-time," she said.

Melville asked, "Has Moshe been part of the Resistance for a while now?"

"Only since his brother Ben was arrested," she said.

Captain Melville looked at a report in the manila folder on his desk and said, "According to our reports, you're referring to Benjamin Yosef. Am I right?" he asked.

Sybil nodded and said, "Yes, Benjamin Yosef is Moshe's older brother. I never met him. I only knew what Moshe told me about him."

"How did you get involved with the raid that took place

this morning," Melville asked. Sybil started to explain but her emotions took over and she cried. Through her tears, Sybil explained, "Moshe was so angry about his brother being in prison. He convinced me to go with him to the meetings. We talked about the raid but he promised me that no one would get hurt. It was just talk, he said. I didn't think that anyone would get hurt."

Melvile asked "Did you know that we lost a man in the raid on the fort today?"

Sybil seemed surprised. She started to cry as she said, "I am so terribly sorry. I never meant to hurt anybody. I feel so ashamed."

Melville knew that this was an innocent girl caught up in a bad situation. Unfortunately he also knew that he had to proceed with what he had to do. Melville said, "Now look, Miss Hargrove. You and your associates came on this property with intent to commit a violent act against the Crown and the people of Palestine. I have no choice but to turn the case over to the prosecutor's office for further action."

With that he asked the guard to return Sybil to her cell. What Sybil didn't know was that her whereabouts had been known and tracked since her capture yesterday morning. It was before 8 o'clock on Tuesday, 5 February, when Ted Hargrove got the call in his office. It was Richard Greaves, the administrative aide in the High Commissioner's office. "Morning, Ted, it's Richard Greaves. I have some troubling news. It seems your daughter Sybil was part of an underground group that attacked the Ramat Gan weapons depot this morning."

Ted was shocked. He had trouble comprehending the words as Greaves was telling him. Richard put him at ease, saying, "Please let us know how we can help you and your daughter." He thanked Richard and said he would call him back within the hour.

Ted knew what he had to do. He made two calls in quick succession. First, he called Millie at home. After quickly explaining the details as he understood them, and trying to calm her down, Ted asked Millie to stay at home near the phone. He promised her that he would stay in touch. His second call was to his personal attorney, Todd Brewster-Armstrong. Todd said he would immediately work on the case and would be back on the telephone with Ted within the hour.

True to his word, Todd, his long-time friend and attorney, called him back before an hour had passed. Todd said, "Sybil got herself in quite a jam, Ted. She was a participant in a violent act and, unfortunately, there was a fatality."

The news stunned him. He asked Todd, "Can we get her out on bail while all of this gets sorted out?" Todd said he would be in touch with the High Commissioner's office as well as the Prosecutor for the Crown and would see what he could do.

Hours passed. Ted went home to be with Millie. Both of them were so distraught over the entire matter. Ted's usual "stiff upper lip" attitude and mentality clearly were replaced with a loving, worried concern for his "Syb" and "Mil." It was 4:45 pm when Todd called Ted back at home.

"Ted, here's the best I could do," Todd said. He explained, "It could be as much as ten days or more before this matter will go before the High Commissioner's Office, Ted."

"But Todd, I'm an officer in the High Command administrative unit," Ted pointed out. "Naturally, I assumed that this matter could be expedited."

"Sorry old boy," Todd replied. "You should know how

bogged down they are." He added, "But when her case comes before the High Commissioner, and the fact that their office knows you and your service to them, in all likelihood Sybil will be released to your custody in your capacity as an officer of the Protectorate, Ted." Ted wanted to say thanks then, but Todd quickly stopped him and said, "Unfortunately this matter is far from over. Sybil will have to remain at home until the court inquest and may face criminal charges before the Crown," he added.

Ted and Millie both got on the phone and thanked Todd for all of his efforts.

It was Wednesday, three weeks later, before 8 am, when Ted, Todd and Millie went to the fort. After signing the necessary paperwork, and waiting for what seemed an awfully long time, a security officer brought Sybil out to them. She was dressed in the clothes she was wearing when she was arrested. Her hair was disheveled and she knew that she needed a bath badly. But Sybil was so happy to see her Mum and Dad and their family friend, Todd, that she wept with relief. Ted thought to himself that at least the worst of this ordeal was resolved for the moment. But he knew that tough times were ahead.

The following week, Ted surprised Millie and Sybil early on Wednesday morning. It was Millie's birthday and he announced, "Well, we're all going out. So put on your finest afternoon finery."

"Going out?" Sybil asked. She could hardly contain her enthusiasm. While they were dressing, first Sybil, and then Millie, asked where Ted was taking them.

After all of the turmoil and upset in their lives lately, Ted, Millie and Sybil were happy to get dressed in their best clothes and were ready to go into the car in 45 minutes. Ted stepped into the car, then turned in his seat, took in a deep breath and told Millie and Sybil where they were going. "We're having luncheon and tea at the King David Hotel," Ted said. Sybil said she had heard about it, but with all the fuss and madness her Dad made about his offices that were situated in the southern wing of the hotel, she had never set foot inside it. Millie had been there several times and said she always marveled at the hotel's ruby red rose stone walls and how neat and clean the hotel seemed to be.

Waiters dressed in crisply starched jackets and dress pants embroidered with the hotel name were neatly and efficiently serving this afternoon's luncheon and high tea patrons. The waiter who was serving them, Alex, recognized Ted as an official in the High Commissioner's office and gave him a broad smile. Ted ordered lamb chops, medium well. Millie ordered a chicken breast plate and Sybil did as well. Iced tea and ice box cookies brought luncheon to a conclusion. Sybil, Millie and Ted had a most marvelous meal and knew that their luncheon at the King David Hotel was something they would always recall.

Chapter 11

In a prison the news travels fast. It was probably the middle of the afternoon, Benjamin thought. Through his cell bars, listening to guards and the others talking, and from what he could gather, it sounded like it could be his brother, Moshe, and others in the Ben Yehuda cell who had attacked, were captured, and wounded in a raid on the fort at Ramat Gan. But there was no way to be sure until Benjamin's next meeting with Itzhak—due to happen any day, he thought to himself. But he couldn't be sure. He had lost any sense of time sitting in a cell. He thought that it must be more than six months since he had been captured, manacled and began his new existence in a six foot by eight foot cell.

Life had gotten harder, he thought. Benjamin was worried about how his family was doing without him. His farming regularly brought in some money and some food for the table. Often, in his sleep, Benjamin would recall times at home with his brother; he loved to roughhouse with Moshe. They would argue, talk about sports, and even though he hated to admit it, Benjamin loved it when his brother gave him a hug. He loved to tease and tickle his sister Becca until she yelled. And sometimes when he didn't expect it, Becca would jump on his back and want to be carried around. And then there was his Mama. She seemed tired most of the time. She watched other families' children, sewed, and even worked at the nearby farm collective herself just so that her own children could have food on the table and a better life. It had been hard for his Mama without Papa. Oftentimes at night, when she thought everyone was asleep, Sara would cry; sometimes in her sleep she would call out her husband's name. "Avram! Avram!" and then there would be a mournful wail. For the most part those memories brought a smile...and then sometimes Benjamin would remember the hard times and he would taste salty tears.

Most of the time he felt so alone. He hoped that his family thought about him, too. "How could Moshe let himself get involved?" Benjamin asked himself. And yet, secretly, Benjamin was proud of his brother and the risk he took. All in the name of the Resistance, he thought. If it was Moshe....

Every day seemed like the one before. It was early morning when two guards came to Benjamin's cell. "Prisoner...Yosef..." one yelled. Benjamin could hear the voice. He didn't move fast enough. While one guard stood watch, the other guard took his rifle and nudged Benjamin with it and said, "Get on your feet, prisoner." Benjamin quickly complied, turned around, was shackled, and led to the area where prisoners could meet with their counsel. It was Itzhak.

Itzhak watched as the guards brought Benjamin in, freed his wrists of their handcuffs, and then went and stood directly behind Benjamin. While not too surprised, Itzhak saw that Benjamin had lost a lot of weight. His face had a sickly pallor to it and his eyes seemed sunken in his face. Itzhak knew the rules—there was to be no physical contact between visitor and prisoner. So he merely waved an outstretched hand and nodded his head in Benjamin's direction.

"How are you, Benjamin?" Itzhak asked. Benjamin looked at Itzhak and gave a short nod. "I wish I had good news for you Ben," Itzhak said. Benjamin's eyes opened wider as Itzhak told him about Moshe's participation in the raid on the fort at Ramat Gan. "Your brother's been badly hurt," Itzhak noted. "Will he live?" Benjamin asked. "All we can do is hope," Itzhak added.

Benjamin asked about his mother and sister. Itzhak reassured him that they were both doing as well as they could under the circumstances. Then Itzhak brought up the matter of Benjamin's continued imprisonment. "I have asked for a meeting with Colonel O'Dowell of the British High Command," Itzhak said, "so that I can get a better understanding of where this matter stands. I will be back to see you as soon as I know more," he said. There wasn't much else to say. Benjamin thanked Itzhak for coming.

Once Itzhak left the visitor's area, the guards shackled Benjamin and brought him back to his cell. Back in his cell a wave of emotions enveloped Benjamin. For the first time in weeks he felt more hopeful about his future and yet, at the same time, he felt upset about his brother Moshe's situation. As he headed back to his office, Itzhak thought about getting on the appointment calendar of a High Command functionary. It wasn't ever easy, he thought, but sometimes it was a necessary evil.

Ted Hargove knew that he loved his daughter, Sybil, very

much. He also knew that she had fallen in love with a boy named Moshe, had gotten herself and the boy tangled up in the Resistance movement and, on top of that, had participated in an ill-fated attempt to take over the Ramat Gan munitions fort.

Now Sybil was home. During these past few weeks she had put on a "brave" front, waiting to see if she would be called in by the Crown's Prosecutor for an inquiry, deposition, and possible trial. Sybil tried to stay hopeful and busy at home, mostly by helping her Mum with the cooking. Sybil also tried to knit, but without much success. Sybil's dad didn't say much about some of the dinners that she had cooked, but it was clear that her cooking skills were not nearly as good as her Mum's. Mostly, Sybil was bored and pined for Moshe. She daydreamed about him many times during the day. She had some of her chums from school over, and Ruthie from the bookstore came on her day off to keep her company. The girls sat in Sybil's bedroom, gossiping and laughing. They looked through old issues of *Photoplay* magazine and talked incessantly about the stars—Judy and Mickey and Clark Gable. There was always lots of news in the gossip columns to talk about, and it helped to take Sybil's mind off worrying about Moshe and his medical condition. Ever since that day when Sybil and Moshe were captured and separated, she thought about him, dreamed about him, and yearned to hold him, to feel his arms around her, to stroke his face and kiss it. She was hoping that Moshe was feeling better, but had no way of knowing how we was feeling, since there was no way to communicate with him in the hospital.

Sybil knew that she couldn't ask her Dad about Moshe. He was reluctant to talk about the whole matter of the Resistance, let alone talk about her strong feelings of love for the boy. What was it, Sybil wondered, that made it so hard for her and Dad to have a civil conversation about Moshe? The first time Sybil brought it up, her Dad overreacted as he usually did on matters concerning her. She knew that she would have to bring it again up sooner or later.

Over the last few weeks, Ted had been wrestling with his own feelings about this Jewish boy, Moshe, who loved his daughter. From an early age on until he reached 21 and moved on to university, Ted was subjected to his father's frequent rants against the Jews, the Nazis and the "royals," amongst other items on his Dad's "sour grapes" list. "You can blame most of the troubles in the world on the Jews," his father often said to Ted when he lived at home with his Mum and Dad. His mum did her best to steer clear of the heated conversations between father and son and tried, as much as she could, to be the "peacemaker" when their tempers flared.

Ted had always been a top student in primary and secondary school, so it didn't come as a surprise to his family and friends when he was awarded a scholarship to attend King's College in London. It was in university when Ted developed his interest in history and government. In his first year of studies, he joined the students' International Club and there met people of different nationalities and religions, and widely expanded his circle of friends. Ted found that he enjoyed studying about various religions, too. After a term learning about the Jewish people and their 5000-year history, he seemed intrigued. The Jews that he met and studied about seemed to be some of the most decent, honorable people he knew.

It wasn't until his father took ill and needed Ted's help that Ted Senior and his son had a chance to sit down and talk openly and honestly. Ted finally was able to tell his father how uncomfortable he was with his Dad's insensitive and hurtful comments, especially about the Jews. Uncharacteristically for him, Ted Senior apologized and told Ted Junior that he knew that he needed to be more tolerant. Within a year of their conversation and improved father-and-son relationship, his Dad passed away. He was in his early sixties and left this life far too soon, Ted Junior thought to himself.

The anger and animosity that Ted had felt towards his stubborn, cantankerous Dad had been released. Or so he thought. But a Jewish boy interested in dating Sybil? Maybe even marrying her? It was something that Ted had to face and deal with.

What Sybil didn't know, and Ted hadn't told her, was that almost from the day that Sybil was released from prison to his custody, Ted knew that he had to meet Moshe and had arranged to make it happen. Through his supervisor's office authorization, and with the full support and cooperation of Itzhak Gamel, Ted was granted permission to make a visit to the medical ward of the Ramat Gan prison. It wasn't more than a 45-minute drive to the fortress. Ted parked, showed his identification to the sentry at the front gate, and was admitted to the facility. He parked his car and walked up to the medical wing of the fort. Once inside, he had to be patted down by a guard as a security precaution.

The area looked old but was clean, Ted noted to himself as he entered the lobby. An old elevator brought him up to the second floor. Ted walked to a desk where a guard was stationed. He showed his ID and was asked for the name of the patient he wished to see. Ted told the guard Moshe's name. The guard muttered something as he looked up the name in a big, handwritten ledger on his desk. So much protocol, Ted thought. There was a strong smell of disinfectant that permeated the air.

"Twenty minutes is all you've got," the guard said. "Give me the pass back on your way out," he added, as he gave Ted a handwritten slip of paper with the patient's name and bed number written on it.

As he left the guard station and entered the ward, Ted could hear some moaning, obviously coming from some of the patients. He walked down the row of beds, looking at the bed number at the foot of each bed. As he did, he noticed that some of the patients were asleep, some were staring blankly, while others were smoking and chatting with their fellow patients. As Ted came to Bed 12 on the South Wing, he saw a tall, skinny young man lying there, one wrist shackled to the bed.

"Moshe? Moshe Yosef?" Ted asked.

"Yes?" Moshe answered.

"I'm Sybil's Dad, Ted Hargrove."

Moshe looked at Ted and said, "I didn't think that anybody knew where I was or what happened to me."

As Moshe spoke Ted felt a strong connection with this young man. He reached out and patted Moshe's hand and asked, "How are you doing?" Moshe gave a slight smile as Ted said, "We've all been worried about you. Sybil especially."

Moshe asked "How is Syb doing?"

"She's fine. And home with her mother and me...I have spoken to Mr. Gamel and he told me all about what happened. Look, Moshe, I know you're a young person who got caught up in a messy situation." Moshe nodded his head and listened as Ted explained, "I'm going to work on getting you released from this hospital. I know that you were shot, but fortunately the bullet grazed you. No real damage, he added."

"How are my mother and sister and brother doing?" Moshe asked.

Ted said, "Your mother and sister don't know I'm here to see you. They've never met me. I hope to let them know that you're alright and we'll see what we can do to get you home to them." Ted looked more glum as he said, "Your brother…" but then the guard informed him that visiting time was over.

"Stay strong, Moshe," Ted said. He shook Moshe's hand and left. For the first time in a long time Moshe felt hopeful as he turned over in his bed as best he could. He closed his eyes and tried to visualize today's events in his mind. He was asleep quickly.

The next few weeks proved to be fruitless, as far as Ted was concerned. If he thought that gaining Moshe's freedom would be easy, he found that the opposite was true. Besides having to file paperwork with the Crown's Prosecuting Attorney's office detailing the crime committed, explaining the reason for a conditional release under supervision for Moshe, Ted had to have paperwork drawn up describing his involvement in the matter and approval by the High Commissioner for Palestine.

Enough paperwork to last for a lifetime, Ted thought.

It was nearly a month later when Ted received notice that Moshe would be released to his supervision. It was then, and only then, when he knew for certain, that Ted told Sybil. Of course, Millie knew weeks before that Ted was working on Moshe's release but she promised Ted to keep it a surprise until he was sure that Moshe would be conditionally released. It was 7 am on the 12th of May, an overcast morning, when Ted presented himself in the administrative office at the

Ramat Gan Fort to pick up Moshe. The processing of the release was a fairly quick and straight-forward matter, Ted thought. By 8:30, with Moshe in the car, Ted drove to his home on Ben Yehuda Street in Jerusalem.

Millie greeted Moshe with a "hello" and a kiss on the cheek. Sybil was still in her bedroom, getting dressed. Ted said, There's someone I know who will be very happy to see you. Shall I call her in?" Moshe nodded. "Syb, can you come in, please?" Ted asked.

A minute or so later, yelling as she was headed to the living room, Sybil was saying, "Good morning, Dad. What are you doing home…?" She never even finished her question because as soon as she came bounding into the living room, there was Moshe standing there, smiling at her. "Oh Moshie," she cried as she threw herself into his arms. They hugged and kissed and Sybil's tears of joy brought smiles to everyone's faces.

After giving Sybil and Moshe a few minutes alone, Millie fixed scrambled eggs with toast and jam and hot tea and everyone ate. As they sat in the dining room eating and talking, Ted said, "I love my daughter very much, Moshe. I only want her to be happy. I've gotten to know you and I can see that you're a good man. I know that you two wanted to be together. Well, Millie and I accept that and we'll be there for you." It was at that point that Sybil, tears in her eyes, went over to her Dad and her Mum and hugged both of them. Ted shook Moshe's hand and added. "I just want both of you to know that you have a tough road ahead of you. No doubt that you will certainly have a court appointment, maybe an inquest, and maybe even a trial," he added.

There was an awkward silence for a little while everyone

finished their breakfast and thought about what Ted had just said.

Then Ted said to Moshe, "Why don't you call up your Mother and let her know that you're here. Tell her that you've been released to our custody, that you're staying with us for a while, and if she would like to come over, I'll bring the car over, pick her up, and bring her over here for a visit." There was no answer at the Yosef apartment when Moshe called.

It wasn't until later in the day when Moshe called again and Sarah and Rebecca were home. Rebecca answered the telephone. "Moshie, is that you?" she excitedly asked.

"Yes, it's me. Is Mama home, Becca?" he asked.

"Where are you?" she asked.

"Put Mama on, Beck. I want her to know everything that's going on." Sarah came on to the phone. She cried as she heard her son's voice.

Briefly, Moshe told his mother about the conditional release and that he was a guest of the Hargroves for the time being.

They agreed to meet at Sarah's apartment that evening. At 6 o'clock, Ted and Millie Hargrove, their daughter Sybil, and her boyfriend Moshe Yosef, got in the car for the short drive to Sarah's apartment in Jerusalem.

He felt funny about using his key to get into the apartment, so Moshe rang the bell. On the first ring of the doorbell, his 14-year-old sister Rebecca was there to open it. "Oh Moshie!" she yelled, and gave him a big hug. She saw Sybil and hugged her, too.

"Hi, Becca," Sybil said, and gave her a hug.

Sarah stood there in the foyer. Then she came over to her son, kissed him, hugged him and didn't seem to want to let go.

Rebecca said "Mama, this is Moshe's girlfriend, Sybil. Or I should say 'his wife'?"

Sybil quickly replied "No, Becca, it didn't happen. We didn't get married." Then, facing Mrs. Yosef, Sybil said, "How do you do, Mrs. Yosef? I'm very happy to finally meet you." They just stood there for a moment, looking at each other. Then Sarah took Sybil's arm in hers and walked her and the others into the living room.

"Please sit down and make yourselves comfortable," Sarah said.

Ted said, "Now Mrs. Yosef, Millie and I and Sybil and Moshe, of course—we wanted to come over and talk to you about this situation."

"We were pretty sure that nobody came over to talk to you or to tell you what had happened," Millie added.

Sarah asked, "What did happen? I heard very little—only some bits and pieces from the lawyer, Mr. Gamel, and whatever was in the letter that Moshe left for us." She turned to Sybil and said, "So suppose you tell me what happened?" Sybil looked at Moshe, who smiled and encouraged her to explain.

"Well, that night...the night we left, we didn't really have a very good idea of where we were going," Sybil said. "Oh, we had some big ideas, that's for sure. We talked about finding a Rabbi to marry us...we also talked about staying at a really cozy place for our honeymoon but we didn't know where to go. I had sensibly packed some things in my overnight. Moshe had a duffel with some things but we really didn't have much else," she added.

And money...did you have any money? So what did you do?" Rebecca asked.

"Moshe said he knew a place where we could stay, have a

meal, and help out. So he took me to meet his new friends," Sybil explained.

Mrs. Yosef asked, "New friends? What friends? From the university? I don't understand."

"They meet in a warehouse. It's a Resistance group formed to fight for the free state of Israel," Moshe explained.

"They were happy to see us. We had a place to stay….food to eat," Sybil added. Sybil hesitated, but Millie intervened.

"Well go on, dear," Millie said. "Tell Mrs. Yosef and Rebecca the rest of the story."

Sybil said, "Yes, Mum. Now this is the part that I'm sorry about. But they were all talking…Telling us how they were going on an adventure. They asked us to help. Hold open some doors, carry some boxes, stuff like that. I went along with it," Sybil said.

"I did too," Moshe added. "We wanted to be part of the group," he added.

"We wanted to do something that would make a difference," Sybil noted.

Ted said, "They didn't realize, or maybe she just didn't understand, that they and their "new friends" were staging an attack on the Fortress. They were all arrested. Because I'm in the Office of the British High Command, I got a call. They were holding my daughter. Well I hurried there, had to make a few phone calls but was able to get Sybil released to my custody."

Mrs. Yosef asked, "And Moshe?"

Ted said: "Well, it took some doing and it took some time, but I made the case that these were two innocent youths caught up in something they hadn't planned and I was able to get Moshe conditionally released to me, pending an inquiry and possible trial."

Mrs. Yosef asked, "You did that for my son?"

Ted said, "Yes, but we have a long road ahead of us before this gets resolved."

Chapter 12

It was a typical Monday morning in early March,1946, rainy and chilly.

The staff members at British High Command offices had clocked in nearly an hour and a half ago. Everyone knew Monday mornings meant Colonel Kenneth O'Dowell was meeting with his staff in his fourth floor office and conference room. What hadn't been typical, but were becoming more frequent, were the anti-British attacks by members of the Resistance.

Over the past year and a half, the Resistance had been actively carrying out missions that were aimed to sabotage or destroy British operations—nothing was safe in their reign of terror—from raids on British radar installations, to sabotage of British sea vessels and the bombing of Palestine's railroad network. Most recently, Operation Markolet or, as they were calling it the "Night Of The Bridges," was carried out by the Haganah. The latest reports showed the destruction of eight bridges that connected Palestine to its neighbors Lebanon, Syria, Jordan, and Egypt.

"We lost a lot of prestige with that raid," O'Dowell told his officers. "While the damage reports are still coming in," he said, "the toll was in the area of 200,000 pounds sterling." Outwardly, with his "stiff upper lip" attitude, he didn't show more than a business-like attitude towards these incursions and terror attacks, but inwardly Ken O'Dowell's "gut" told him that the pace and severity of these attacks would only get worse.

It was an hour since the meeting began, O'Dowell noted to himself. He wrapped up the meeting, thanked everyone and returned to his office. As he sat at his desk, Ken could hear classical music softly playing on the radio in the outer office, occasionally interrupted by the radio announcer with the news. His aide, Major David Lester, could be heard typing on his Remington typewriter. The phone rang, and Major Lester quickly answered it. A moment later, he stuck his head in the office and said "Ken, a lawyer named Itzhak Gamel is here to see you."

"Gamel? Itzhak Gamel? What does he want?" O'Dowell asked.

"He's the counsel for Benjamin Yosef. He wants to talk," Lester replied.

O'Dowell said "About his terrorists, no doubt." He thought about it for a moment and then added, "All right, send him in." A moment later Itzhak Gamel was ushered into O'Dowell's office.

"Itzhak Gamel," Major Lester said as a way of introduction to O'Dowell.

"Have a seat, Mr. Gamel," O'Dowell said. "Now, what I can do for you? My aide didn't tell me the purpose of your visit today."

Gamel said, "Let's dispense with the pleasantries, Colonel."

O'Dowell didn't even look up. He already knew what Gamel came for, and as far as he was concerned, putting on his Sunday "go-to-church" manners for Gamel and his "bunch" wasn't his style.

"I'm sure that the Crown has notified you of my appointment to represent David Bruner," Itzhak said.

"Yes, Mr. Gamel, I have been notified," O'Dowell said. "So?" O'Dowell asked, and stared at Gamel with a hard, cold stare.

Itzhak Gamel stared back and said, "I have asked that the Crown's case against Benjamin Yosef be merged with that of David Bruner's."

O'Dowell said, "So I understand." But it was clear that the matter was unresolved as far as Itzhak was concerned, for he stood up, took a few steps and said, "Look Colonel, you and I both know that my clients have been sitting in a jail cell for close to three months now. As their counsel, I demand to know when their cases will be tried. Or are they going to continue to sit in their cells at Acre?"

Very cooly, O'Dowell replied, "Oh, come now, Mr. Gamel. You better than anybody should know that these matters take time. The court's slate is quite filled. Perhaps in another month we'll have a better idea of when the case will proceed."

Itzhak started to respond but O'Dowell, seeing that he had the opportunity, said, "Now, about these terrorists......"

"They're prisoners, not terrorists," Itzhak quickly replied.

"Yes," O'Dowell said, as he reached over to get a folder on his desk, take a paper out of the folder and read it.

"Benjamin Yosef. Imprisoned for shooting at British soldiers with intent to kill. A very serious crime. Life imprisonment— maybe even the gallows," he said.

Itzhak looked at him, disbelieving what he was hearing. "The gallows? Why we both know that these charges aren't true. Yosef didn't shoot at the soldiers. He shot one bullet into the air."

O'Dowell replied "I don't know if they're true or not. I wasn't at the scene of the crime, Mr. Gamel, and neither were you."

"Benjamin Yosef has told me the truth. I believe him," Gamel said.

In a mocking, sarcastic way, O'Dowell replied, "I'm very glad to hear that, Mr. Gamel." Continuing, Colonel O'Dowell said, "Let's look at the facts. A Jew, Benjamin Yosef, armed with a pistol, walks down the highway. A truck carrying British soldiers, and clearly marked, at that, comes along. Yosef fires one bullet at the truck for no apparent reason. He is standing in a perfect position to fire a shot and wound or kill a soldier riding in the truck." He paused for a moment, staring at Gamel and said, "An act of terrorism. He will have a fair trial."

Gamel asked, "Where? And when? You haven't filed any charges yet. There's been no notification."

O'Dowell leaped to his feet and said, "Benjamin Yosef will appear before a court of British Military Law. He may have any counsel that he desires and as many witnesses as he wishes. And, as for the date of the proceeding, you will be notified as soon as possible."

Both men stood staring silently at each other for a few moments. Itzhak watched as O'Dowell sat down, took papers from his desk blotter, not paying attention to him at all.

Itzhak stood silently watching O'Dowell for a moment or two more before he sat down, facing O'Dowell. "And what about Lieutenant David Bruner?" Gamel asked. "Where does his case stand?"

In a quiet voice O'Dowell replied, "Frankly, I'm very surprised that he's still alive. The guards at the fortress were tempted to kill him rather than just wound him. He too, will have his day in court."

"That's fine," Gamel said. He paused for a moment and then added, "There's one other matter that we need to resolve."

O'Dowell, still working at his desk, looked up at Itzhak and said, "Yes, Mr. Gamel. What is it?"

Gamel, still seated, facing O'Dowell, said, "Lieutenant Bruner told me that he is entitled to receive his salary from the Army for the last two months of service to the Crown."

O'Dowell rose from his chair, anger clearly in his face, walked around the desk until he was standing next to Gamel, leaned into him, shaking his finger at him, and asked, "My God, man. Do you think we are going to pay a defector, a traitor to the British?" Almost immediately O'Dowell realized that his temper had gotten the best of him. He returned to his seat, smiled at Gamel, and in a firm, business-like manner, said, "You will have to excuse me, Mr. Gamel. I've got a lot of paperwork to get through today. My aide will escort you out."

"See you in Court, Mr. Gamel," O'Dowell said, as Major Lester came in and escorted Gamel out. Once he was sure that Itzhak Gamel had left, O'Dowell called in his aide, Major Lester, and said, "Look, Les, first of all, this Gamel, who's defending Yosef and Bruner—He's clever, shrewd. He's going to do his best to free those Jews. Make sure you don't say anything to him. The less he knows, the better. And if he comes in again, I'm not in. Is that clear?

"Yes, sir," Major Lester replied.

Major Lester turned to exit, but there was one more thing that O'Dowell wanted him to do, as he said, "Now listen, Herm. I want you to give Bruner his back pay."

Lester looked at the Colonel for a moment, then said, "Bruner? He's one of them."

O'Dowell said "That's right, Les. I want him to receive every cent."

"But Ken, he's a turncoat," Major Lester said. "You're going to pay him for being a traitor?"

O'Dowell said, "That's the way I felt until this lawyer, Gamel, walked in. Then I realized that this will confuse them. They're testing us. Let 'em think that we're going to be as lenient as hell with Bruner and Yosef. The surprise will come in court."

"What about the complaint and the trial?" Major Lester asked.

O'Dowell said: "I know, Les. We've been keeping it close to the vest. They'll have their day in court and counsel of their choice and all the witnesses they want."

Major Lester asked, "But what happens if they're exonerated. What if the judge sees the evidence for what it's worth and sets them free or gives them a reduced sentence?" O'Dowell gave his aide a look and a smile as he said, "Now look, Herm, It could happen, but it won't. Military trials are interesting that way."

"I don't understand, sir," Major Lester said.

"You will soon enough," O'Dowell said. "You know, the Resistance has played right into our hands. Now Britain's occupation looks right in the eyes of the rest of the world. I think the more we can play up this terrorist angle, the more assured of a conviction we'll be," he added.

Major Lester said, "But their defense at the trial might be brilliant and the ruling might prove favorable to them."

"It could conceivably happen, Les," O'Dowell said, and smiled at both of his aides. "We'll just have to wait and see."

Chapter 13

As he walked along the tree-lined streets of Jerusalem's Kiryat Shmuel neighborhood, Itzhak Gamel purposely stopped a couple of times to breathe in a few relaxing deep breaths before reaching his destination and the tension and angst that he knew would surely be awaiting him. He was deep in his own thoughts, and so it came up so suddenly— the former St Antonio Monastery, taken over by the British during World War II—now the Supreme Military Tribunal for the Protectorate of Palestine.

After his years in law, there weren't too many events that surprised him, he thought. Even so, it had been less than a month since his contentious meeting with Colonel O'Dowell about the continued imprisonment of Benjamin Yosef and David Bruner without a firm trial start date. And now here it was —Day 1 of the trial—today, Tuesday, April 2, 1946.

The past month had proven to be an an extremely hectic time with all of the pre-trial paperwork, meetings with his clients, Ben Yosef and David Bruner, in addition to keeping up with his leadership activities for the Resistance effort, while attempting to stay on top of his burgeoning law office caseload.

Something had to give and he knew it. The late nights and early morning hours were catching up with him, and Itzhak felt incredibly weary. After completing the security check-in in the main lobby, he took the crowded elevator to the second floor courtroom. Itzhak presented himself to the Chief Military Justice for the trial, Captain David Willis who, in turn, introduced him to Lieutenant Arthur Lloyd, representing the Crown.

After a brief "sidebar" with the barristers and the Judge, each defendant was escorted into the courtroom flanked by an MP at each arm, unshackled, and seated at the defense table. It shouldn't have come as a surprise, but even Itzhak was taken aback at how pale and gaunt David and Ben seemed to be as they sat down.

"Attention. All rise," the Court clerk said. "The Supreme Military Tribunal for the Protectorate of Palestine is now in session. The matter before this Tribunal is the Crown versus Benjamin Yosef and David Bruner. Chief Justice David Willis, presiding. Please be seated," he added.

Everyone sat and immediately turned their gaze toward the front of the room and looked to the Chief Justice of the Tribunal.

Tall, slim, handsome were not the words usually associated with a member of British jurisprudence. But in this case, they more than adequately described 60-year-old David Willis, referred to by colleagues and adversaries alike as "Chief." He said, "This trial will be conducted according to legal procedures set forth in the manual of the British Military High Command. All questions, evidence, procedure and decisions are to be duly referred to and considered by me."

Almost immediately Itzhak Gamel rose to his feet and said, "Your Honor, the defense moves for a postponement of this proceeding."

"Objection, your Honor," Captain Arthur Lloyd said, representing the Crown. Bespectacled, with a growing middle-age paunch and thinning white hair, Arthur Lloyd seemed more like a middle class office worker than Chief Prosecutor for the Protectorate. Shrewd, cunning, and extremely thorough, his reputation for winning cases was legendary.

Captain Willis asked, "On what grounds does the Defense ask for a postponement?" Gamel said, "Insufficient time to prepare a proper defense, Your Honor. We need additional time with the defendants to develop a thorough case." Willis replied, "Motion denied. The prosecution may begin its opening statement."

Arthur Lloyd rose to his feet and said, "Thank you, Your Honor. The prosecution will prove that David Bruner and Benjamin Yosef have, by the nature of their unlawful acts, perpetrated high crimes against the British government, protector of Palestine under the Balfour declaration. We will prove that Benjamin Yosef, a citizen of the protectorate, did, on 7 January 1946, shoot a pistol, with malice and premeditation, at a clearly-marked British Army truck carrying officers and soldiers. We will also prove that on Wednesday, 20 February 1946, David Bruner, a soldier in the British Army, who was wooed by bribes and a commission to the Resistance, a terrorist organization, led an attack on a British supply fortress. By leading the attack he committed treason under the provisions of the Army Act of 1881. Both of these men, without concern for life, breached the laws of the British occupation government with barbaric and terrorist actions.

And it is the recommendation of the prosecution that these traitors to the Protectorate and mother country should receive the death penalty with no recommendation for clemency."

There was total silence in the courtroom. Itzhak looked over at David and Benjamin and gave a nod. Both Bruner and Yosef swallowed hard. Itzhak had expected this. He patted Ben's hand and gave a reassuring smile.

Justice Willis looked in Itzhak's direction and said, "Mr. Gamel, you may present the opening statement for the defense."

Itzhak rose to his feet. "Thank you, Your Honor. The Defense will concede that Benjamin Yosef fired a bullet on the day in question. But the Defense will prove that the shooting was not a pre-meditated act and that the bullet was fired, in a spontaneous act, in the air. The Defense will concede that David Bruner participated in an action at the arms fortress at Ramat Gan. But we will prove that he did this not as a citizen or soldier of the Mother Country, but as a member of the Jewish community. The defense will admit that a crime was committed but the charge of traitor is not justified or valid."

Itzhak sat down in his chair, feeling very satisfied with how his opening statement, the first leg in the journey, went. But he also knew that this would be a steep, uphill climb.

"Captain Lloyd, the prosecution may begin its case," Justice Willis said.

"Thank you, Your Honor. The prosecution calls as its first witness, Sergeant Richard Benson," Captain Lloyd responded.

A tall, thin military man, with wavy black hair, walked to the front of the room, stepped into the witness box and was sworn in by the court clerk. "Now, Sergeant Benson," Lloyd began. "Will you please explain where you were on the day in question, Monday, 7 January 1946, at approximately 11:45 am?" he asked.

Benson replied, "Yes sir. I was riding in the back of the supply truck as it rode down the main highway in Ramat Gan."

"A military supply truck?" Lloyd asked.

"Yes, sir," Benson replied. "I command the eight men in that squad."

Lloyd asked, "What was the weather like on that day?"

Benson replied, "It was sunny, sir. A bit chilly, I recall."

"In which direction was the truck travelling?" Lloyd asked.

Benson answered, "East, sir."

"Were there any obstructions that would block your view of the highway as you sat in the back of the truck?"

"No, sir," Benson quickly answered.

Lloyd asked, "How fast was the truck going as it travelled along?"

Benson said, "Not fast, sir. Probably about 30 kpm."

Lloyd said, "Please tell the court what you saw as the truck travelled along the highway."

Benson said, "Well, as I was saying, I was sitting in the back with the others when I saw a fellow was walking along the side of the highway in the opposite direction. As we passed by him, he lifted up his pistol and aimed the pistol right at us. Then he fired."

Lloyd said, "Let me stop you right here, Sergeant, and ask you to look around the courtroom." Sergeant Benson stood up in the witness box, looked past the prosecution table and fixed his eyes on the defense table. Lloyd continued, "Do you see the gentleman who was walking at the side of the highway, walking in a westerly direction, at the time and date in question?"

Benson said, "Yes, sir, I do."

"Will you please point him out to the Court."

Sergeant Benson pointed to Benjamin Yosef and then sat down.

Lloyd said, "Let the record indicate that the witness is pointing to Benjamin Yosef." In a curt, yet efficient, manner, Captain Lloyd said, "Thank you, Sergeant Benson. I have no further questions for this witness."

Justice Willis turned to face Itzhak Gamel and said, "You may cross-examine the witness."

"Thank you, Your Honor," Itzhak replied. Continuing, he said, "Tell me, Sergeant Benson, besides yourself, were there many soldiers seated in the back of the truck?"

"Yes, sir, about forty others besides me," Benson replied.

"Did everyone have room in the back of the truck, or was everybody cramped?"

Lloyd jumped to his feet, saying, "Your Honor, I object. This court, I'm sure, is not interested in the comfort of the British soldiers in the back of a military truck. Where is this leading us?"

Gamel said: "Your Honor, I have a relevant point to make here."

Willis said, "Objection overruled. You may proceed, Counselor."

"Thank you, Your Honor," Itzhak said. "Tell me, Sergeant, were there any soldiers seated in front of you in the back of the truck?"

Benson seemed puzzled and asked, "In front of me, sir?"

"Yes, Sergeant," Itzhak said. "You said that the truck was crammed in the back with seated soldiers. At any time during the ride down the highway, could any one of those soldiers have blocked your view?"

Benson said, "Well, the truck was crammed, and my mate, Eddie…I mean Sergeant Carruthers, came over, sat next to me, and we talked."

"Did you have to move over to give Sergeant Carruthers room to sit down?"

"Well, yes, I did," Benson replied.

"And at approximately what time did the Sergeant move over next to you?"

"When?" Benson asked, rhetorically. "I can't remember exactly when."

Gamel asked, "Then is it possible that you didn't have a clear, unobstructed view of someone walking by the side of the highway at 11:45 in the morning?" There was no response. So Gamel asked again "Well, is it possible?"

"Objection," Lloyd said.

"On what grounds?" Justice Willis asked.

Lloyd answered, "Badgering the witness."

Justice Willis said, "Overruled. You may continue, Counselor."

Gamel said, "So again, let me ask you, Sergeant, is it possible that you didn't have a clear, unobstructed view from the back of the truck at all times?"

Benson said, "Well yes, sir, I guess so. But I heard the shot fired."

"Tell me, Sergeant Benson," Itzhak asked. "Is it possible that the sound that you heard was that of a pistol being shot in the air?"

"Well, I…yes, it's possible," Sergeant Benson admitted.

"Thank you, Sergeant. No further questions."

Justice Willis excused the witness and said, "Prosecution may call its next witness."

In a loud voice, Lloyd said, "The Prosecution calls Benjamin Yosef to the stand." A much thinner and older-looking Benjamin Yosef walked to the stand. After he was sworn in by the Court Clerk, Benjamin sat in the witness box, awaiting a tough questioning by Chief Prosecutor Lloyd. He didn't have to wait long.

"Now, Mr. Yosef, will you tell the court exactly where you were and what you were doing on the day in question, Monday, 7 January 1946, at approximately 11:45 in the morning," Lloyd asked.

"Yes, sir," Benjamin replied. "I was walking along the Ramat Gan Highway. I was carrying my pistol," he added.

Lloyd asked, "Your pistol?"

"Yes, sir."

"Where did you get it?"

"It was my Papa's. I've had it many years."

"Do you have the papers at home to prove it's yours?"

"Probably," Benjamin replied.

Lloyd asked, "Were you ever questioned about the pistol?"

Itzhak Gamel jumped to his feet, saying, "Objection!"

"On what grounds?" Justice Willis asked.

"Counsel for the Crown has failed to establish a foundation for questioning the defendant about the pistol ownership," Itzhak Gamel replied. It was clear that counsel for both sides needed a ruling, so Justice Willis asked both sides to meet in his chambers to present oral arguments. The trial was recessed until 9 am the next day.

The day had been long and arduous for Itzhak but, in retrospect, he felt that his case for David and Benjamin had gone about as well as he could have predicted. Arthur Lloyd was pleased at how well he had managed to present a clear-cut case for the Crown.

And the chance to see her Benjamin meant so much to Sarah. Seated next to her in the courtroom were Moshe and Rebecca and Sybil and Millie Hargrove.

In the early evening after the first day of the trial, sitting at his cluttered desk in his Ben Yehuda Street law office, Itzhak had a chance to think about the day's events in greater detail. The prosecution's opening statements were as crisp and succinct as he knew they would be. Surprisingly, the question of the pistol—its ownership and registration, and the uncertainty as to its use by Benjamin (whether fired with malice or not) left Itzhak with some confidence that there was a possibility—granted it was a slim one—but a possibility nevertheless, for a short prison term or perhaps even an acquittal for Benjamin.

Benjamin Yosef hated the courtroom and the inevitable confrontations that lie ahead. He viewed himself as more of a "take charge" kind of person. Having to explain himself—to answer the "why" wasn't in his nature, he thought. It wasn't until after lunch on the second day of trial when Justice Willis said "Mr. Gamel, the defense may begin direct."

"Thank you, Your Honor," Itzhak said. "The Defense calls Benjamin Yosef," he added. After he was sworn in, Benjamin sat in the witness box, nervously looking around. Itzhak smiled at him ever so briefly and then said, "Now Mr. Yosef, please tell us, in your own words, the events that occurred at 11:45 am on Monday, 7 January 1946."

Benjamin said, "Sure. I was walking along the main road in Ramat Gan. I had my pistol with me. I saw a truck pass by me. I noticed it was a British truck. I fired one bullet in the air."

Gamel asked, "Why did you fire that bullet?"

"I don't know. I just did," Yosef replied.

"How did you know that it was a British truck?"

Yosef replied, "By the seal on the side of the truck. It's the Union Jack."

"Did you know that the truck was a military truck?" Gamel asked.

Yosef said, "No. I can't say I did."

"Didn't you see the designation "Army" below the seal?" Itzhak asked.

Yosef said, "No sir, I didn't. The truck was going too fast."

Itzhak said, "I have no further questions for Mr. Yosef."

Justice Willis asked, "Any re-direct, Captain Lloyd?"

"Yes, Your Honor," Captain Lloyd replied. Court observers who knew him marveled at the persuasive ability of Chief Prosecutor Arthur Lloyd. His no-nonsense approach in questioning of witnesses was so effective that there was little doubt that he would be obtaining a conviction quickly. Unlike Itzhak Gamel in his rumpled suit and wind-blown hair, Captain Lloyd's hair was neatly combed, his suit was well-tailored, and he maintained an even disposition no matter what happened in the courtroom.

Captain Lloyd walked over to the witness stand, looked at Benjamin Yosef, nodded to him, and said, "Good afternoon, Mr. Yosef."

Benjamin Yosef nodded his head. Captain Lloyd said, "Now, please tell the Court where you live and what you do for a living."

Benjamin replied, "I live in Rosh Pinah."

"Do you live there by yourself?" Lloyd asked.

"No. I live there with my mother, my brother and my sister," Benjamin replied.

"And what sort of work do you do?" Lloyd asked.

"I work in the fields."

"Do you own a car?"

"No, I don't," Benjamin said.

"So how did you get to Ramat Gan?" Lloyd asked.

Benjamin said, "A friend of mine drove me."

"What's the name of your friend?" Captain Lloyd asked. As he did, he leaned in towards Benjamin, as if to emphasize the question.

"Ellie," he replied.

"His last name, please," Captain Lloyd said, a little more emphatically.

"Stern. His last name is Stern," Benjamin said.

"How do you come to know Ellie Stern? Do you work with him? Or is he your neighbor?"

Ben looked at Captain Lloyd for a moment and hesitated before he replied. "No, he's not. I just know him, that's all," Benjamin said.

"How do you know him, Mr. Yosef?" Lloyd asked. But before Benjamin could answer, Captain Lloyd leaned in and asked, in an insistent tone, "Is it possible that you know him through the organization you belong to—the Resistance?"

Itzhak Gamel jumped up quickly and said: "I object!"

"On what grounds, Mr. Gamel?" Chief Willis asked.

"Leading the witness," Gamel responded.

Chief Justice Willis said, "Sustained. Please refrain from leading the witness, Captain Lloyd." Lloyd nodded his head. Chief Willis said, "You may continue your examination, Captain Lloyd."

"Thank you, Your Honor."

Everyone in the Court watched while Captain Lloyd calmly walked over to the Prosecution table, looked at some notes he had written on a yellow legal pad, put the pad down, spun on his heel and said, "Now, Mr. Yosef, I would like to go over a few points about your recollection of the events of Monday, 7 January 1946."

"Yes, sir, " Benjamin Yosef replied.

"Does thirty kilometers per hour seem fast to you?" Lloyd asked.

"No. Not really," Yosef answered.

"And yet you couldn't read the lettering on the truck as it drove past you?" Lloyd asked. "You couldn't tell that it was an Army truck?"

"Well, yes," Benjamin Yosef replied. "I couldn't."

Captain Lloyd took a step towards the witness box and said, "Tell me, Mr. Yosef, could you tell that men were riding in the back of the truck?"

Yosef said, "I wasn't paying any attention. You see, when the truck passed I quickly lifted my pistol and fired a shot off."

Lloyd leaned his body in and asked, "You knew that the truck was British?

Yosef said "Yes."

"You fired a bullet off for no apparent reason. Is that what you're saying?" Not even waiting for Yosef to reply, he continued by asking, "Now tell me, why would you or any man for that matter, go to a town where they don't live, walk along a busy road during the morning rush, take a pistol, and fire a bullet into the air and not at a target?"

"I don't know, sir." Yosef replied.

"Let me ask you this, Mr. Yosef. If a man has a cause he believes in and he wants to make a statement—doesn't it seem logical to you that he would fire a shot into the air?" Captain Lloyd asked.

"I object, Your Honor," Itzhak Gamel quickly replied.

Willis asked, "On what grounds, Mr. Gamel?"

Gamel replied, "Counsel is conjecturing and badgering the witness."

Justice Willis said, "Sustained. Stick to the facts presented, Captain Lloyd." There was a pause and a hush in the courtroom while Captain Lloyd again consulted his handwritten notes at the prosecution table.

After what seemed like an eternity to Benjamin, but really just a few minutes or so, Captain Lloyd turned, faced Benjamin, and asked, "Tell me, Mr. Yosef, how often have you taken a car ride with Mr. Ellie Stern?"

"Just that one time," Benjamin replied.

"And why ask Mr. Stern to drive you?" Captain Lloyd asked. "Were you just looking for a way to spend the day along the highway with a friend or did you have something more specific in mind?" He didn't wait for an answer and then asked, "Did you ask Mr. Stern to stay or did he go off, leaving you by yourself?"

Benjamin stared and said, "I asked him to leave me and go."

Itzhak thought about objecting, but it was clear that Lloyd had effectively made his point that this was not a pleasure ride with a friend but a definite journey with a specific plan in mind. Captain Lloyd rose and said, "Your Honor. I have no further questions for this witness."

Justice Willis asked "Any re-direct, Mr. Gamel?"

"No, Your Honor," Itzhak Gamel replied.

"The defendant may rejoin counsel at the defense table," Justice Willis said. Benjamin felt a great sense of relief as he crossed over to the defense table. On the way back to his seat, he looked over the courtroom gallery where his mother, brother, sister, Sybil and Mrs Hargrove were seated. This time he smiled at them.

The trial was adjourned until the following day.

Itzhak gave Benjamin a hug and some reassuring words. He shook hands with David Bruner as the court officers who had been standing in the back of the courtroom walked over to the two prisoners, shackled them, and then led them away. Itzhak looked at his watch. Still early enough for him to call home, he thought. Then maybe a quick bite before going back to his office and tackling the mound of paperwork lying on every table and desk that never seemed to get smaller.

It was the third day of the trial of "The Crown vs Benjamin Yosef and David Bruner," Thursday, 4 April 1946.

After some morning preliminary business, Justice Willis convened the trial at 10:00 am. The court clerk called David Bruner to the stand, and after Bruner was sworn in and seated in the witness box, Itzhak Gamel rose to address the court. "Your Honor, Mr. Bruner wishes to have no defense but his own," Gamel said. "I am, with your approval, Your Honor, resigning as Mr. Bruner's counsel."

Justice Willis asked David Bruner, "Is that your choice, Mr. Bruner? To be your own counsel, and for Mr. Gamel to withdraw as your counsel?"

David Bruner stood in the witness stand, turning to face Justice Willis, saying, "Yes, Your Honor. I am not allowing Mr. Gamel to represent me because I wish to speak for myself."

Chief Prosecutor Arthur Lloyd rose and said, "I must object, Your Honor. This procedure is highly irregular."

"Overruled," Justice Willis replied. "Since Mr. Gamel has dismissed himself as Mr. Bruner's counsel, then Mr. Bruner has a right to represent himself as he sees fit. I will ask, however, that Mr. Gamel remain as a legal advisor to Mr. Bruner. Is that satisfactory to you, Mr. Gamel?"

"Yes, Your Honor," Itzhak replied.

"And to you, Mr. Bruner?" he asked David.

"Yes, Your Honor," Bruner replied.

Justice Willis said, "Good. Then you may proceed with your opening statement, Mr. Bruner."

David Bruner turned to face Justice Willis as well as much of the gallery and said, "Thank you, Your Honor. I wish to go on record as saying that I do not recognize your right to judge me."

Arthur Lloyd immediately jumped to his feet, saying, "I object, Your Honor."

"On what basis?" Justice Willis asked.

"This is not a proper opening statement," Lloyd replied.

Justice Willis said, "While the statement is not in proper form, I will permit the defendant to make his statement. Prosecution's objection is overruled. You may continue, Mr. Bruner."

"Thank you, Your Honor," David Bruner said. "As I stated before, this court has no lawful right to exist. You have come here to correct the greatest injustice ever inflicted upon any nation, but you make us the world's foremost victims of persecution and massacre. You are determined to transform this country into one of your military bases, one of many— and to steal it from the people who have no other home in the world than this. You have no right to be here. The Hebrew youths are fighting and will continue to do so, until you return it to its lawful owners—the people of Israel."

"Your Honor, I object. These inflammatory remarks should be stricken from the record," Arthur Lloyd said.

"I understand your objection Counselor," Justice Willis

said. "But in view of the fact that Mr. Bruner has not consulted with Mr. Gamel to prepare a proper statement, I will allow Mr. Bruner's statement to be admitted into the record."

"Thank you, Your Honor," David replied.

"You may call your first witness, Mr. Bruner," Justice Willis said.

"I have said all that I wish to say. My statement speaks for the way I feel," David Bruner said.

"Do you wish to cross-examine Mr. Bruner," Justice Willis asked Arthur Lloyd.

"Yes, Your Honor."

"You may proceed."

"Thank you, Your Honor. Mr. Bruner, did the Resistance officials offer you any money or a commission to encourage you to join their organization?"

"I have nothing to add to my statement, Mr. Lloyd," Bruner replied. Arthur Lloyd stared at David Bruner, but David was careful to avoid Lloyd's direct gaze.

Lloyd took a few steps closer to the witness box, leaned in, and in a more insistent tone asked, "Now did you join the Resistance before or after you renounced your British citizenship? Isn't it true that you met with a top Resistance official while you were an officer in the British Army?"

Bruner quickly replied, "Again, sir, I have nothing to add to my prior remarks."

Justice Willis said, "The defendant will answer the prosecuting attorney's questions or else I will hold him in contempt. Do you understand, Mr. Bruner?"

"Yes, I do, Your Honor. My statement speaks for itself. If you wish, you may hold me in contempt of court," he added.

Justice Willis said, "Mr. Gamel, I will give you time to

meet with the defendant and advise him as to the consequences of his actions."

"Yes, Your Honor," Itzhak Gamel replied.

Justice Willis called a recess until that afternoon. In the interim, Itzhak Gamel was able to meet with David Bruner and then, afterwards, the MPs placed Bruner in their custody and shackled him until the court was ready to reconvene. When the court officer was notified that the Judge was ready to reconvene, both Benjamin Yosef and David Bruner were brought back into the courtroom, unshackled, and seated at the defense table.

Like every day at the trial, seated in the gallery were Sarah Yosef, her son Moshe, her daughter Rebecca, Moshe's girlfriend Sybil Hargrove, and her mother Millie. Millie knew to be quiet and observe the court proceedings. Sybil did her best to comfort Moshe and to act like a big sister to Rebeca, whose crying could be heard throughout the second floor of the justice building. Sarah tried to control her emotions as best she could. She tried to remain stoic for Benjy's sake, but at home the brave front crumbled and her wails of anguish were almost incessant and non-ending.

It wasn't until 2:30 when the Justice's gavel reconvened the session.

"All rise! Court is now in session. The Crown vs. Benjamin Yosef and David Bruner. Captain David Willis, presiding," the court clerk said. "You may be seated," he added.

Justice Willis said, "A verdict has been reached in this case. But before rendering that verdict, this court declares contempt of court charges against the defendant, David Bruner. Mr. Bruner, you will rise and face the Bench. You are hereby sentenced to a period of one month in the Fortress of Acre to be credited to time already served."

A slight smile crossed Itzhak's face when he heard this part of the verdict. But inwardly he knew that this would probably be the only positive outcome in today's proceedings.

Justice Willis continued, "David Bruner and Benjamin Yosef, you have been found guilty as charged, of attempted murder and of perpetrating high crimes of a treasonous and traitorous nature against the British Occupation government. It is the decision of this court that no recommendation for clemency be granted to you. Therefore, David Bruner and Benjamin Yosef, you shall be transferred to the death cell at the Fortress of Acre. And on the fifteenth of November in this year of 1946, you shall be hung by the neck until dead. And may God have mercy on your souls."

Quickly the guards surrounded the prisoners, handcuffed and shackled them and led them away.

As the verdict was being declared by the Judge, Itzhak Gamel looked around the courtroom and could see many Resistance members seated in the gallery. Many in the courtroom jumped up, yelling, "We shall appeal this sentence! Our brothers shall not go to the gallows! We shall appeal! We shall appeal!" The shouting continued unabated. Justice Willis tried to gavel the crowd to silence but to no avail.

It had been a while since Sarah had been able to see Benjamin. His appearance had shocked her. He lost much weight and he seemed almost listless. When Benjamin saw his mother, he gave her a slight smile and a nod.

Itzhak warned them all that this would be a very grueling trial with an uncertain outcome. What lay ahead? All they knew for certain was that tomorrow awaited them...

Chapter 14

As he usually did on a weekday, Ted rose earlier than Millie or Sybil, showered, shaved, and was sitting in the kitchen in his comfy old robe and bedroom slippers before the grandfather clock in the front room chimed six times. It was a Monday early in July, so Ted knew that he would be wearing his linen suit today.

Seated comfortably at the kitchen table, sipping a freshly brewed pot of Earl Grey while munching on toast and reading the paper, Ted completely lost track of time. Before he knew it, the clock chimed a half past seven. He quickly went into the bedroom and changed into a freshly starched white shirt, his light blue linen suit, conservative blue tie with a pinstripe design, and his freshly polished wingtip shoes. A folded hankie went into the lapel pocket of his suit. Ted stopped for a moment to look at himself in the mirror, and he was pleased.

By now Millie was up, as was Sybil, getting washed and dressed.

Neither one of them paid much attention to Ted as he

scurried around before leaving for work. Sybil had managed to get back her old job at the bookstore with reduced hours, but she was happy to have a place to go to and to be in the company of her girlfriends like Ruthie, who was always a lot of fun.

Millie volunteered her time down at the canteen. She liked talking to the soldiers, hearing about their stories. Most of the men there that day were Brits, temporarily assigned to Palestine but yearning to be across the Pond with their own families. They appreciated her interest in them, even if for only a little while. Millie was good at making "small talk" and she enjoyed spending the better part of Monday and Wednesday down at the Canteen.

"Goodbye, Mil. Have a good day," Ted shouted up to the closed bathroom door as he hurriedly walked out the door to catch the bus 2 blocks away. She yelled back a "goodbye" but wasn't sure if Ted had heard it. The 6-minute walk to the bus terminal and 20-minute bus trip to his office gave Ted a chance to think and also take a short nap.

It was a tough time to be living in Jerusalem, he thought. Especially for a staff member of the High Command Office. Frequent briefings about Resistance groups and their increasingly violent activities had put everyone on edge, and even amongst the general populace tensions had risen over the past year, due in large part to threats of bombings by the Resistance that had been reported on the radio and in the newspaper. In some cases, there were two or three threats received each day. Every one of them had to be documented and investigated by the MPs as well as by the hotel security detail.

Troublesome, Ted thought, as he arrived at his destination, the King David Hotel on King David Street. As he usually did when he reached the hotel, Ted took a few minutes to stop at the Lobby registration desk and say "Good morning" to the clerk on duty before crossing over to the southern wing where the High Command offices were situated. This particular morning there was a larger than usual contingent of MPs and High Command security officers gathered.

Ted nodded to security officer Harold Smythe, crossed over to his office door, and stepped into his office. Olive Whitt-Jones, Ted's personal secretary, already had honey scones and tea service waiting on the sideboard. As a safety precaution, the High Command security office intercepted the mail meant for each High Command officer and carefully screened each letter and package. Olive knew her boss and made it a point to have Ted's incoming mail from yesterday scanned and delivered to his office first thing in the morning, preferably, while Ted was sipping his tea and munching on scones.

Commissioner Cunningham's senior staff meetings regularly convened at half past ten on Mondays and, true to form, started promptly. The most urgent piece of business that had crossed the Commissioner's desk earlier that morning were the three phone calls warning that explosives had been placed in the King David Hotel that would soon explode. The calls were made to the King David Hotel lobby desk, the French Embassy, and the Palestine Press.

High Command security did not pay much attention to these calls. With little else to cover, the senior staff meeting concluded by 12:00 pm. Ted returned to his office. His private secretary Olive requested a longer than usual lunch hour today because she was meeting her brother in town.

Now that the senior staff meeting had concluded, Ted thought, he would also take a longer than usual luncheon break. Millie's birthday was just a few days away and Ted hadn't shopped for her present. If there was one thing for sure, Ted thought, a gift for Millie was always appreciated, but never more than now. The constant bomb threats and tense atmosphere in the office were always on Ted's mind, even though the matter remained unsaid. Ted rang up the sergeant at the security desk to let him know that he and his secretary were taking a one-hour luncheon break today. Ted and Olive exited the office and boarded the elevator. They walked out through the main lobby and said a quick goodbye to each other.

Ted headed up the street to catch the bus. Olive headed in the opposite direction to meet her brother. It seemed like hours, but it was really moments, when a series of loud explosions rocked the hotel and its surrounding area. Ted, thrown to the pavement, shakily stood up. He ran his hand over his face and brushed off fragments of glass. He looked over at the front of the hotel, now a tangled mess of steel, concrete and glass, There, on the sidewalk, body parts were strewn everywhere.

Sirens could be heard coming toward the hotel.

Ted crossed the street, and in a kind of daze, walked over

to the pay phone. He was going to call Millie, but all the operator heard was the dial tone. Ted had passed out.

It was two days later when Ted awoke. He was in a private room of Jerusalem Hospital. Looking down to the foot of the bed he saw Millie, Sybil and Moshe.

"Hello, dear," Millie said. She bent over and gave Ted a kiss, as did Sybil.

In halting words, Ted asked, "What happened?"

"There was an explosion in the hotel," Mille answered. It was obvious that Ted's memory was affected by the blast and, as the doctor explained to Millie later, "your husband has experienced a concussion and he seems shell-shocked."

"What does that mean, Doctor?" Millie asked.

"Mr. Hargove will have to recover from the bomb blast," the doctor replied. He went on to explain what bomb blast trauma can do. "Mr. Hargrove may forget names, places, even people he knew. His mood may be affected, and it will take time for him to recover," the doctor added.

"Do you understand, Mrs. Hargrove?" the Doctor asked. Millie shook her head "yes" to indicate that she understood.

"What happened?" Ted asked. "Why am I here?"

In a matter of fact tone, Millie explained "they blew up the King David Hotel. It's pretty bad," she said. Ted nodded his head. "Close to 100 are dead or missing," Millie said. "They've been working on the site for the past two days," she added.

Ted shook his head. Just then he recalled saying goodbye to Olive and watching her cross by the triangle of Jaffa Road, Ben Yahuda Street and King George Road on the way to meet her brother. Ted seemed agitated as he said Olive's name. "Olive. What's happened to Olive?" Ted asked, as he tried to sit up in bed.

Sybil quickly answered, "She's fine, Dad. She had turned the corner when the bomb went off." Millie fluffed up the pillows on the bed. She could tell that Ted was very agitated. He wanted to do more than lie helplessly in bed, but she wouldn't let him.

Meanwhile, emergency meetings were being held throughout government offices to denounce the bombing. At first Ted thought that he would be back in his office in no time at all. But he saw himself that his recuperation was taking time. Truth be told—Ted's injuries from the blast and his brain injury were more severe than first recognized. The doctors were in agreement with Millie and Sybil that Ted should retire from his post. In his mind and heart, Ted knew that he would never return to his office.

Chapter 15

During this trial Irgun activity had continued without a stop. Irgun fighters had planted bombs that detonated at British headquarters in Tel Aviv. In March, an explosion in British headquarters in Haifa resulted in seventeen deaths. Other Irgun fighters had been responsible for the explosion in the British embassy in Rome.

The pace of bombings had quickened—and became relentless. There were two bombings one day apart in September, an attack on four British policemen in a bank robbery by Irgun Resistance fighters, and an attack on a British police station. The Alhambra Cinema in Jaffa was the next target for Irgun bombs. During the period of December 11 through 16, eight actions were organized and carried out by the Irgun Resistance fighters, ranging from bombings at the Damascus Gate in Jerusalem to Palestinians and others wounded or killed in the Haifa police station.

The date selected for a large Irgun attack was Saturday, the first of March 1947. The target selected was a British Officer's Club in Jerusalem. As dusk was falling, the fighters got into their positions, standing ready at 2325 Herzl Street, around the corner from their target—number 2300. In advance of the others, three fighters sneaked up to the target just as the first set of explosive charges detonated. They were caught in the melee. By then the remaining charges detonated. The fighters, who were now standing in their attack positions, fired their rifles and threw their grenades.

Moshe thought of himself as being a good man, a hard-working Jew, but at this particular time he felt that he was carrying the weight of the world on his shoulders now. Six months ago he had broken up with his girlfriend, Sybil Hargrove. It was over something silly, he thought. He wanted to stay home and she wanted to go out. He noticed that Sybil always had pocket money, and most days he couldn't come up with enough for the bus. This upset him, too. Moshe's mother and sister lived in an apartment in Tel Aviv. He was living with two roommates in an apartment in Jerusalem.

Sybil and Moshe's relationship had its ups and downs. She had her own apartment, subsidized by her parents. Sybil had been working for the lawyer, Itzhak Gamel. Also, she could draw down from an allowance that her father, Ted, a former Palestine government official, had set up for her. They tried to see each other on weekends, but most days, life and finances proved to be difficult. They patched things up, or so Sybil thought, until three days ago, when Moshe's jealousy and controlling ways came up in conversation. Sybil had accused Moshe of becoming possessive of her and her life. "You keep me from seeing my friends," she said.

"Of course I don't," he replied angrily. Sybil recalled how Moshe would want to know who she was talking to and about what. Things had gotten worse, she recalled, recounting the details of their argument to her mother. "Moshe wants me to tell him about every person I meet and talk to all day long," Sybil explained.

"Everybody?" Millie asked.

Sybil shook her head "Yes," and as she did, she started to cry.

Millie was not one to go into displays of affection, but she could see how upset her daughter was. She went over and gave Sybil a hug. "What he's asking you to do is not normal," Millie said. "He has to trust you,"' she added.

"I know, Mum," Sybil said. "What should I do?"

Millie thought about it and said, "Talk to him. Tell him that he is being unreasonable. I'm sure he will listen to you." She makes a lot of sense, Sybil thought. She decided to bring it up with him after dinner tonight. She thanked her Mum and sent her home. Sybil cooked a nice dinner for Moshe and herself. They ate their meal of meatloaf, potatoes and string beans sitting in silence in their kitchen.

What happened next was not what Sybil expected. As she finished drying the last of the dinner dishes she said, "I need to talk to you, Moshe."

"What about?" he replied, with a touch of anger in his voice.

"Your attitude," she said. "You're being unreasonable, expecting me to tell you about each and every person I talk to each day," she added.

"Oh, is that so?" he said, storming over to her and standing menacingly.

"You look like you're angry, Moshe," she said. "Don't sulk."

"Maybe I am angry," he said. "I want you to do what I tell you," he said.

"I don't have to," she replied.

"You really frustrate me," he said, grabbing her wrist and twisting it. His anger was mounting. Sybil tried to get away from him. She screamed at him, which only got him angrier. He applied more pressure to her wrist. She finally yanked her wrist away from him and started to run from the room, but he had more arm strength than she did. This wrestling infuriated him. He stormed over to her, punched her in the eye, and then in the jaw. Sybil collapsed to the floor—and passed out. Moshe stormed out of the apartment and slammed the door.

It seemed like a minute, but it was more like a half hour later when Sybil awoke and groggily tried to stand up. The whole room was spinning. She collected herself and when she was sure he had left, she shakily dialed her Mum's phone number.

"Mummy, Moshe hurt me," Sybil said, weeping.

Millie could hear the upset in her daughter's voice. "I'll come right over, honey," Millie told her.

Forty minutes later Millie entered the apartment. It looked like a tornado had hit it. Furniture was upended, pictures of Sybil and Moshe that were neatly arranged in picture frames on an end table were ripped and torn to shreds. Millie found Sybil crouched on the floor, crying, while looking at the ripped pictures of happier days that she and Moshe shared.

"It's all quite a mess, isn't it?" Sybil asked her mother, as Millie helped her get off the floor.

"You've got quite a shiner there," Millie said, looking at Sybil's swollen bruised right eye. Millie knew what to do. She applied a bag of frozen peas to Sybil's eye. She also saw and knew that Sybil's swollen black and blue jaw would hurt like hell. "I think it would be best if you come home with Dad and me," Millie said.

"No, Mum, I can't," Sybil replied. "I've just got back to my secretarial job with Mr. Gamel," she added. Millie felt nervous, but Sybil insisted on staying in her apartment with Moshe's things still there. Reluctantly, Millie left her daughter's apartment and headed home. She felt that this wasn't the end of Sybil's problems with Moshe.

Two nights later, a very drunk Moshe came to Sybil's apartment. His key for the front door didn't seem to work. He didn't know that Sybil had a new key made so after several attempts to get in, he stood under her second floor kitchen window and yelled. He also pounded on the front door to no avail. After half an hour he left. Later that evening he called Sybil but all he did was to curse at her and threaten to beat her up some more. She let him yell his head off.

It was a week later. Her injuries, shiner and black and blue skin hadn't disappeared as she had hoped. But Sybil wasn't dissuaded so easily. She remembered the kind, gentle and sensitive boy who won her heart. The Moshe she knew was goofy, funny and kind-hearted. Even though she knew she didn't have to, Sybil tried to reach out to Moshe.

He wasn't having any part of it. Her phone calls to him were not returned and the two letters she wrote to him just a few days after the fight were not opened and returned.

Sybil called Sarah Yosef, Moshe's mother, and was able to talk to her on the telephone. She didn't tell her about their fight.

Sarah told Sybil that Moshe had recently joined Haganah. Some called it the "Stern Gang." "It's the military, like the Irgun," Sarah told her.

"Why, are you worried?" Sybil asked.

"He's been acting crazy," Sarah added.

Sybil asked her, "Crazy? What do you mean?"

Sarah replied, "I mean he comes in most nights so mad, so angry, that he throws things around and destroys things in the apartment. I can't talk to him."

Sybil knew, from her own experience fighting for the Irgun, that shooting a rifle, fighting battles, and defending a position from an attacking enemy could change a man like Moshe. More than anything else, what Moshe felt was a combination of boredom and a fear of the unknown. Originally, he went down to the Haganah's local recruiting drive because his buddy, Ezekiel (everybody called him "Zeke"), was going down to join up and he was going to keep him company. But once Moshe met some of the fighters and talked with them he was convinced that this group was for him. He really liked it that the Haganah had been against the British takeover of Palestine. Moshe went home with Zeke and was excited to do his part.

There was required orientation and training before Moshe and Zeke could participate in group activities. His squad spent the first of three days on battle tactics and went on a forced five-mile march. Next, they worked with rifles and marksmanship.

On the second day, there was instruction in the use of machine guns, hand guns and explosives. On the third day, the recruits went on a ten-day march with full gear, and each recruit had to carry out each task on this list:

- Report enemy information on the radio

-Engage targets with an M1 rifle

-Employ hand grenades

-Move under direct fire

-Move over, through or around obstacles

-React to indirect fire

-React to flares

-Camouflage yourself and your equipment

-Personal hygiene in the field

-Firing weapons (Rifle, Bayonet, Machine gun loading, Flares)

-Care of feet

-Evaluate a casualty

After the three days the recruits who passed basic training attended a graduation ceremony. Moshe was advised to see his squadron leader where he would receive further orders.

"You failed to complete the required elements of basic," his squadron leader told him. He asked his leader what he should do now. "You'll be given a chance to re-do the elements that you didn't master," his leader explained. Moshe felt relieved. He found it a struggle to keep up with other recruits when it came to the forced marches with full gear. He knew that he was flabby and out of shape. He decided that he wasn't going to run anybody's race but his own. He was told that he would be assigned to his bunk for two days off and then he would start the re-take of the entire basic training program.

Moshe really tried to do better on the re-take of basic. He especially improved on rifle marksmanship. But at the end of his training, the leader for his squad marked his progress with an incomplete. Moshe thought about his buddy, Zeke, who had passed everything, so he was assured of his place in a squadron.

Moshe didn't know what the next step in his military service would be. He felt very discouraged. But now that he was in this situation, he was wondering who had the responsibility for these para-military agencies. Was it the High Commissioner's office that would be involved in determining his fate? He wondered.

Moshe had contacted his mother about his status. Sara Yosef couldn't appeal to Ted Hargrove since he had officially retired at the end of the year. Besides, Ted had been told by his daughter that Moshe had badly beaten her up in a quarrel.

"I have no sympathy for any man who would strike a woman," Ted said. "Especially since the injured woman is my dear daughter, Sybil," he added.

There was an important decision that Moshe had to make. He had two options: get drummed out of the military or quit. There was only one option that made sense. He would leave. The day after his squadron leader gave him an incomplete for his basic training re-do, he left the squadron's headquarters in Tel Aviv early in the morning and travelled on the bus to surprise his Mama in her apartment in Jerusalem.

He knew that he didn't have the squadron leader's permission and the completed paperwork to make this trip. He would have to face the consequences when he got back to headquarters. For now Moshe wanted to hug and kiss his Mama and taste her cooking and let her fuss over him.

Sara Yosef was shocked to see her son standing there at her apartment door. "I thought you were in the Haganah," his mother said, eyeing him suspiciously. She reads me like an open book, Moshe thought to himself.

On the bus trip over he had thought about and came up with a believable lie to tell his mother. "I'm on a special assignment from headquarters, Mama," he said. She looked at him with a disbelieving look, but let him finish his story. "And that's why I don't have to go back any time soon," he added.

"I never heard of anything like this," Sarah said. "Are you in some kind of trouble?" Moshe couldn't look at his mother as he said "no" to her question.

She put the phone into Moshe's hand, saying, "Don't you think you owe Sybil an apology for your awful behavior?"

Moshe called Sybil and, after saying "Hi, Sybil" into the phone receiver and, hearing silence, he said, "Look Syb, I want to apologize to you for the horrid way I treated you," he said. She grunted. It was all that Sybil was willing to say in response to Moshe's phone call apology. She recalled the beating and was still as sore as hell.

Moshe knew that he wouldn't be hearing from Sybil any time soon. He knew he had to get going. He imagined that the paperwork for the "AWOL" had already been issued and that the military police were hot on his trail. Moshe said his goodbye and was out of his mother's apartment by two o'clock in the afternoon. He was afraid that he would be spotted on the streets of Jerusalem.

If only he could hide out where he would be safe. He knew that his stupid, impulsive acts had alienated his ex-girlfriend, Sybil, her parents, and her current boyfriend, Marshall. Then it occurred to him. He could talk to Itzhak Gamel. Since he was already in Jerusalem, he figured it would be a short bus ride to Ben Yehuda Street and Mr. Gamel's office.

He called his mother and told her that he was hoping to

see the lawyer Itzhak Gamel. Moshe was very afraid that he would be seen and recognized by somebody walking on the street. He kept glancing over his shoulder as he walked. On the bus over to Mr. Gamel's office, he kept his shirt collar pulled up and tried not to make eye contact with any of the other passengers. When the bus stopped at Ben Yehuda Street, Moshe walked up two blocks, crossed an alley, and crossed over two blocks to throw off anybody who was following him. Then, when he looked around and didn't see anybody who seemed to be following him, he crossed over to be on the block for Mr. Gamel's office.

Moshe was so jumpy now, and had been ever since he walked off from his post and went to his Mama's apartment. It was a mistake that he hadn't thought through before he did it—an impulsive move that he knew he would regret later. Moshe took the stairs to Mr. Gamel's office on the second floor of 15 Ben Yehuda Street, Jerusalem. He pressed the doorbell but didn't answer the intercom when Gamel's secretary asked for his name. The second time he rang the doorbell but didn't answer the bell when the secretary asked, Itzhak himself stepped in to see who was ringing the bell but not answering. Moshe said his name when Itzhak shouted, "Who's there?"

Itzhak gave out a yell of recognition when he heard Moshe loudly say his own name over the intercom. A moment later Itzhak bounded out into the office foyer to hug Moshe and bring him into his private office. "How are you and how is Sybil?" he asked Moshe.

Moshe, looking very dejected, said, "We're not together any more. We broke up a month ago."

"That's too bad," Itzhak said. "She's a very good person. I'm very fond of her." Moshe shook his head in agreement.

Itzhak could see that Moshe was very upset. "I see that you're upset and assume that you need my help," Itzhak said. Moshe nodded his head in agreement. "So please don't leave any detail out, and tell me in your own words what you recall," Itzhak said. "I'll be writing a detailed summary which my secretary, Alice, will transcribe," he added.

Moshe told Itzhak everything that he remembered: the argument with Sybil that led to the brutal beating he gave her, flunking out on his basic training test and re-test, and then being so aggravated at his test that he left and went to see his mother.

"That's all you remember?" Itzhak asked him.

Moshe said "Yes."

"At any point did you decide to leave and not tell anyone where you were going?" Itzhak asked. Itzhak didn't wait for an answer, but asked the critical follow-up question next: "Did you plan to be absent without leave?" Moshe stared at him blankly. "Did you?" Itzhak asked.

"No, I did not," Moshe replied.

Itzhak stared at him and felt he was telling the truth. Moshe, a scared, confused and tired young man, had made a mistake. But it wasn't a criminal mistake, Itzhak felt. That evening Itzhak agreed to serve as Moshe's attorney. He knew that he would have a lot of work ahead of him to clear Moshe of these serious charges, or, at minimum, see that Moshe had a fair trial and a reduced sentence.

As he did on another occasion, Itzhak brought Moshe to his home and to his wife, Miriam's home cooking. A hot meal and good company were what Moshe really craved and, thanks to Itzhak and Miri, he enjoyed, along with a nice glass of red wine, a wonderful respite from anger and tension that evening in Jerusalem.

The next morning at 7 am, Moshe rode in the car with Itzhak into downtown Jerusalem. They planned to go to Itzhak's office on Ben Yehuda Street to continue their work on Moshe's case. Itzhak spotted two military policemen through his windshield. They were standing at the entrance to his office building outside the garage. As Itzhak's car pulled up to the entrance, one of the MPs stopped him. "Yes, officer?" Itzhak asked. The MP looked into the car and asked, "May I please see your identification and the identification of your passenger?" Itzhak took his mandatory Palestine passport and driver's license and passed it through the driver's side window to the MP, whose name tag on his uniform said "Smythe." Officer Smythe looked at the documents and passed them back.

Itzhak imagined that things would become tense in another moment or so as he took Moshe's Palestine passport and passed it out the driver's side window, saying, "This is my passenger's identification." Officer Smythe took the ID, looked at it, and passed it onto the other MP, whose name tag read "Goodmark." Both men, taking their revolvers out of their holsters, moved towards either side of the car. Officer Smythe asked, "Will both of you please step outside of your vehicle and place your hands over your heads?"

Itzhak and Moshe complied with the instructions of the MPs, were handcuffed, and placed in the back of the MPs' car for the ride to the military police headquarters in Jerusalem. Once Itzhak and Moshe were brought into the headquarters, they were separated. An hour later, Itzhak was brought upstairs to the central booking area and interviewed by Officer Smythe, who said, "Mr. Gamel, do you know why you were placed under arrest and brought down to headquarters?"

Itzhak acted like he was totally innocent and unknowing, and said, "I was driving with this gentleman, Moshe Yosef, to my office when I was stopped and detained."

Officer Smythe asked Itzhak, "How do you come to know Moshe Yosef?"

"I have known Moshe Yosef and his family for years," Itzhak replied. "On more than one occasion he and his girlfriend, Sybil, have come to my home and shared dinner with my wife Miriam and me," he added.

"I did not hear the offense that he is being charged with," Itzhak said. "But I am stating for the record that I am here today as his friend and his attorney," he added.

"Did you know that Moshe Yosef has been placed under arrest?" Smythe asked. "He is a freedom fighter for the Haganah who left his post and is charged as Absent Without Leave," Officer Smythe added.

"No, I didn't know that," Itzhak replied.

"You are free to go, Mr. Gamel, Officer Smythe explained.

"As his appointed attorney, I am requesting that I be permitted to see Moshe Yosef," Itzhak asked. Arrangements were made, and 45 minutes later Moshe, shackled and escorted by two guards, was brought up to the third floor to the client/attorney interview room. The shackles were removed and Moshe sat down with Itzhak.

They went over the timeline of the events that transpired, with particular emphasis on the time from the fight with Sybil to the time when Moshe left to go over to his mother's apartment. "I'm going to submit a motion for the dismissal of the charge Absent Without Leave,'" Itzhak said. "I am convinced that Moshe had not planned to abandon his post."

After his meeting with Moshe, Itzhak was about to go to his office. But just before he did, he left with encouraging words for Moshe, "Don't worry, Moshe. I know that you didn't intentionally leave your post. Now we just have to convince the military court of that fact," he added.

The next few weeks were busy for Itzhak as he worked on assembling his case. He hadn't presented a case to a military court before. He imagined that there were some differences between a jury trial and a military court trial. He had to be prepared and ready. He read a book on the subject of court martials but, in the end, he decided to trust his own instincts.

He lined up character witnesses who knew Moshe from school and work who would attest to his character. Sybil found out from Moshe's mother that he was going before a military court. She asked Itzhak if she could be a character witness for him.

"I know Moshe better than most people do," she told him.

He knew about the fight and decided not to include her on the witness list. It was a Tuesday, three weeks later, when the military court was scheduled to convene.

From what he had learned, and from consultation with a military officer, Itzhak knew that a military trial consists of a military judge, the trial counsel who serves as the prosecutor, the defense counsel, and three military officers who serve as the jury. For Moshe's case a special court-martial was impaneled.

Itzhak was named as a special consultant to the trial

defense since he was not a member of the military. In this capacity he could assist the defense in identifying and preparing witnesses. He, himself, would not testify. Itzhak was relieved that he would assist and not be expected to mount Moshe's defense himself.

On day 1 and on each of the following days, Moshe was brought into the court by two court officers. His shackles were removed and he was seated at the defense table.

Presiding at the trial was Judge Advocate Jonathan Gilbert. He gaveled the proceedings to order. He explained that this was a special court martial impaneled to determine the innocence or guilt of Private Moshe Yosef.

The list of offenses with which Private Yosef was being charged was read by Judge Gilbert. The defendant was charged with being Absent Without Leave from his post from 1700 hours GMT on 10 May 1946. This offense was charged as a misdemeanor.

The trial counsel was Captain Lewis Masterson. The trial counsel made an opening statement. "The prosecution will attempt to prove that the defendant was absent from his assigned post as Second Shift Post Sentry on 10 May 1946 without an approved leave order."

"You may call your first witness," Judge Gilbert said to Captain Masterson.

"Prosecution calls Sergeant Henry Williams to the stand," the Captain said. A balding, heavyset, ruddy-faced man walked up to the witness box and was sworn in.

"Please tell the court your name and rank," the Captain said. He did. "Please tell the court, Sergeant Williams, what your duty assignment was for 10 May 1946."

Sergeant Williams replied, "I was the officer in charge of the shift scheduling for the Haganah–Patrol Duty Roster."

"Who was supposed to be on the shift at 1900 GMT on 10 May 1946?" Counsel Masterson asked.

The sergeant consulted his notes and stated, "The duty roster listed Private Moshe Yosef as the soldier assigned to that shift."

"Was Private Yosef at his assigned post at 1900 GMT?" Trial Counsel Masterson asked the the Sergeant.

Sergeant Williams said "'no" and went on to explain that Private Yosef called later that evening and apologized for missing his assigned shift.

After the sergeant gave his testimony the Defense was given the opportunity to cross examine. Major Oscar Bernstein was the Defense Attorney.

"Tell me, Sergeant, who does the recordkeeping for your shift scheduling?" the sergeant was asked.

"I do a lot of it myself with some borrowed help," he replied.

"Who double-checks the numbers and the calculations, Sergeant?" Major Bernstein asked.

"Why I do that myself," Sergeant Williams proudly stated.

"What happens if there's a mistake? Who double checks and corrects errors?" the Major asked.

"I have a staff sergeant spot checking the work each day," the sergeant answered.

Major Bernstein asked, "Could an error happen that's not caught in the spot checking?"

The Sergeant seemed flustered by the question. "I suppose an error could occur, but it's highly unlikely," he replied.

"I have no further questions for the Sergeant," the Major stated.

"Re-direct of the witness, Your Honor?" Captain Masterson asked.

"You may proceed, Captain," Judge Gilbert replied.

"One additional question, Sergeant," the Captain said. "Is there a calculated accuracy rate for your recordkeeping group's work?" he asked the Sergeant.

"Yes, our recordkeeping group has a 97 percent accuracy rate," the Sergeant replied.

"Fine, thank you, Sergeant," Captain Masterson replied. "No further questions for this witness, Your Honor."

The prosecution rested and Major Owen Bernstein represented the defense. Major Bernstein began with his opening statement. "The defense will prove that the defendant did not abandon his post without leave on 10 May 1946. We will further show that the defendant is a person of good character and high morals as attested to by his friends and neighbors, some of whom are here today. We will further show that the defendant did not leave his assigned post on 10 May 1946 without Approved Leave, as he is being charged, but that he left a message with the duty officer to receive permission to leave his post to go home and attend to his elderly mother."

After the opening statement, the Judge said to the attorney for the defense, "You may call your first witness."

The first witness was Private Moshe Yosef. After Yosef was sworn in by the court clerk, he was seated in the witness box.

The Major asked Yosef for his full name, rank, and branch of service. Yosef replied, "I am Moshe Avraham Yosef, my rank is Private, and I serve as a foot soldier in the Haganah."

The Major asked him, "Where were you on 10 May 1946, Private?"

Yosef said, "I was at my post as a second shift sentry."

The Major asked him, "What are your shift hours, normally?"

"1700 to 2400," he replied.

"Were your hours different on 10 May 1946?" the Major asked.

"Yes, Major," Yosef replied. "I had to take care of my mother and asked to be excused at 1900."

"You submitted your request—and what happened?" the Major asked.

"I thought it was approved," Yosef said. "So I took off for my mother's apartment and didn't think about it anymore. She had some chest pains that night, so I was only thinking about her," he added.

"When did you find out that your leave request was denied?" the Major asked.

"The next day, when I got called in by the Sergeant."

Obviously, Major Bernstein explained, there was a snafu —a miscommunication. "Should Private Yosef be punished for an obvious mistake that he didn't cause?" the Major asked.

At this point Major Bernstein called upon his character witnesses to be ready to testify on behalf of Private Yosef. Three citizens were selected for this role: Itzhak Gamel, one of Moshe's employers, Benyamin Auslander, and Moshe's Yeshiva teacher, Adam Nichendorf, Moshe's friend for more than fifteen years.

The court clerk called each character witness up to the witness box and asked for the record who they were, how they knew Moshe Yosef, and in their dealings with him if they found him to be of good morals, to be honest, fair and trustworthy.

At the end of this character witness testimony, each side gave their closing argument.

The panel of three military officers hearing the testimony and rendering a verdict were Lieutenant Ryan Bochery, Lieutenant William Conover and Captain Herman Hausmann. For three days the panel of justices heard all the testimony, saw all of the exhibits and heard the opening and closing statements of both the prosecution and defense and rendered their decision based upon the fair and equitable application of the law to all parties.

It was the judgement of the panel that:

- Private Moshe Yosef be found guilty of the charge of being Absent Without Leave from his post as Second Shift Sentry from 1700 hours GMT through 2400 Hours GMT on 10 May 1946 with extenuating circumstances due to a medical emergency.

- He is to be fined one and a half day's pay, with no other penalty to be enforced.

- This matter could have been handled more expeditiously if the use of court martials be restricted to cases involving felonies.

- Private Yosef should have asked for and received confirmation in writing with his superior officer that he had been excused from sentry guard duty to attend to his parent's medical health needs.

- In the absence of a properly typed and signed document a memorandum should have been prepared in writing, describing the event/activity that occurred and actions taken. The document should be signed by the shift supervisor and countersigned by the senior officer. The documentation should be maintained in the files for permanent retention.

- No other action is warranted at this time.

Moshe was pleased to have this matter resolved and behind him. He felt grateful to have Itzhak on his side. Itzhak put in a good word, and soon Sybil and Moshe met and spoke for the first time in a long time.

Chapter 16

David Bruner was a student of history—especially the
history of Palestine. He prided himself on knowing
that Britain's support for a Jewish state in Palestine dated back
to the time of World War I and a document he had read
about called the "Balfour Declaration."

After World War I, under a mandate from the League of
Nations, Britain was granted temporary control over
Palestine, since its citizens were considered not ready yet to
govern themselves. From his reading, he knew that Britain's
ultimate goal was to make Palestine a Jewish state within the
British Empire. And he was opposed to it.

David and Benjamin were sure that they would be
hearing from Itzhak very soon. They didn't have to wait long.
By the afternoon of the following day, Itzhak Gamel arrived at
the Fortress at Acre to visit his jailed clients, Benjamin Yosef
and David Bruner.

After he cleared the security screening, he was escorted by
a prison guard to the visitors' area and shown to a seat facing
a floor to ceiling glass partition with a built-in two way

speaker. A few minutes later, Benjamin and David, both shackled, were brought in and seated on the other side of the partition, facing Itzhak. A prison guard discreetly stood watch in the back of the room.

"Shalom, Ben, David," Itzhak said. He looked at them. They seemed even quieter and more subdued than when the verdict was announced. Continuing, he said, "I'm disgusted at what happened in that courtroom. But I've begun working on an appeal."

"An appeal?" a seemingly surprised David asked.

Itzhak answered, "Yes, an appeal. To the High Commissioner's Office—maybe even the Privy Council in London. You weren't given a fair treatment in that three-ring circus of a courtroom. And I really feel that the judgment they meted out was not in proportion to the crimes. I tell you, we must appeal." He added, "It's the only option left if you're to have a chance at all."

David gave a slight smile, and said, "I appreciate your concern, Itzhak, but I cannot and will not sign any such document which asks for clemency or a new trial. I think signing is giving the Brits exactly what they want."

Benjamin asked, "Tell me, why should we appeal?"

Itzhak quickly replied, "It's a standard practice—especially in capital cases."

David said, "But don't you understand. The trial was a propaganda move by the Brits. They make themselves look good in the eyes of the world by saying there are subversive elements in Palestine. They'll say—look at this trial. It gives them the reason to stay here to prevent these elements of terrorism from running rampant. Then they go one step further by allowing us to appeal. That makes them look like merciful people to everyone else. I know how the Brits operate. Don't forget, I've been in their Army for a few years now."

Itzhak turned slightly to look at Ben and asked, "How about you, Ben? Will you sign this appeal?"

"I don't know," Benjamin replied. "A short time ago I would have said yes, but listening to David makes me think twice."

"This might be your last chance," Itzhak said. "I'm not trying to tell you how to live your lives but think it over carefully. This could be your ticket to freedom. I'll leave the paperwork with the guard to give to you."

David said, "Now look, Itzhak. I really believe that a man has to do what he thinks is right. If I sign that appeal, then I'm recognizing the right of the Brits to be in Palestine. I'm saying that they have the authority to try me and pass judgment. But they don't. I said it in court and I'll say it again. They have no legal basis for being in this country. And so I don't sign. My death will be a blow struck against them and all they stand for. That's what it means to me."

Itzhak knew that it was time to go. He said "Shalom" and was escorted out of the visitors' room. A few minutes later the guard took Benjamin and David back to their cell.

Later that evening, Benjamin looked at David and then asked, "What should I do? Do I sign?"

David said, "Look, I can't decide for you. It's your life. You decide what you're going to do with it."

If he stood sideways and stared straight ahead, Benjamin could see the gallows at Acre. Daily, at least once in the morning, and once in the afternoon, he would try to exercise in his cell, by walking in circles—ten times in one direction, then ten times in the other. He often daydreamed of boyhood friends whom he had played with, of his brother and sister, and of carefree days, when he said, "But it isn't easy. I look out the window each morning and can see the sky and feel the fresh air. I remember—watching the old men as they go to pray in the synagogue…seeing young children dancing and singing, going off to school. Life! I see life and I want to be a part of it. I don't want to die. And yet, when you talk about a free Israel - a dream that my family has dreamed about for so long, I'm torn. The thought of swinging from the end of a rope, dying at the hands of a hangman. My God! My God! What do I do?"

Benjamin's emotions got the best of him and he started to cry. David went to his side and hugged him.

"It isn't easy, Ben," David said. "No one ever said it would be. You're young and still have the zest and zeal for life. So do I. But now you have to commit yourself," he added.

Benjamin said, "I thought I knew what I was doing when I read that speech to the other Resistance members about taking action. Now I can see how stupid and foolish I was."

David left him alone for a while. A decision like this is not an instant one.

Later that evening Benjamin, sitting in his cell, very still and quiet for the last few hours, put his hand on David's shoulder and said, "I have made my decision. You have given me the strength to say I will not sign an appeal. Let our deaths serve as a reminder to all our Jewish brothers to fight against the oppressor and never give in."

It was a sweet moment as they embraced each other, and David said, "My brother. I'm glad that you've decided as you have."

Benjamin looked at David and smiled.

David said, "You are a brave man, Ben."

On schedule, the lights in the prison went out. As he laid

down on his bunk, David thought that It had been a long day but a momentous one, too.

Friday, the 14thof May, 1948: clouds hung over Tel Aviv as Hirschl Rosenbaum started his daily routine with his morning ritual—putting on the Tefillin and reciting his morning prayers. Then a little breakfast, and he was set.

As a journalist for Haaretz, he knew he had the biggest story of the year. He walked to his car, got in, and drove to the paper's office. He had a couple of hours to kill, but that was all right.

At 2:30, Hirschl changed into a white shirt, tie and sports jacket.

His excitement building, he drove to the Tel Aviv Museum. He, like many others, had been told about the "secret"—that the declaration of independence would be publicly read and signed today! As he entered the room, Hirschl looked to his left and noticed that the radio technician from Kol Israel was setting up his broadcasting equipment. Almost instinctively he looked at his watch and noted that it was a few minutes before 4:00. Seated at the head table of the dais, Hischl noted, was David Ben-Gurion.

Chapter 17

"**E**xactly at 4 pm, David Ben Gurion stood up, stepped up to the podium, beneath a large portrait of Theodore Herzl, and pounded his gavel to call the proceedings to order.

And he said, "WE HEREBY DECLARE that as from the termination of the Mandate at midnight, this night of the 14th and 15th May, 1948, and until the setting up of the duly elected bodies of the State in accordance with a Constitution, to be drawn up by a Constituent Assembly not later than the first day of October, 1948, the present National Council shall act as the provisional administration, and shall constitute the Provisional Government of the State of Israel.

THE STATE OF ISRAEL will be open to the immigration of Jews from all countries of their dispersion; will promote the development of the country for the benefit of all its inhabitants; will be based on the precepts of liberty, justice and peace taught by the Hebrew Prophets; will uphold the full social and political equality of all its citizens, without distinction of race, creed or sex; will guarantee full freedom of conscience, worship, education and culture; will safeguard the sanctity and inviolability of the shrines and Holy Places of all religions; and will dedicate itself to the principles of the Charter of the United Nations.

THE STATE OF ISRAEL will be ready to cooperate with the organs and representatives of the United Nations in the implementation of the Resolution of the Assembly of November 29, 1947, and will take steps to bring about the Economic Union over the whole of Palestine.

We appeal to the United Nations to assist the Jewish people in the building of its State and to admit Israel into the family of nations."

Continuing, he said, "In the midst of wanton aggression, we yet call upon the Arab inhabitants of the State of Israel to return to the ways of peace and play their part in the development of the State, with full and equal citizenship and due representation in its bodies and institutions—provisional or permanent.

We offer peace and unity to all the neighboring states and their peoples, and invite them to cooperate with the independent Jewish nation for the common good of all.

Our call goes out to the Jewish people all over the world to rally to our side in the task of immigration and development and to stand by us in the great struggle for the fulfillment of the dream of generations—the redemption of Israel.

With trust in Almighty God, we set our hand to this Declaration, at this Session of the Provisional State Council, in the city of Tel Aviv, on this Sabbath eve, the fifth of Iyar, 5708, the fourteenth day of May, 1948."

Ben Gurion sat down.

Immediately, an impromptu singing of "Hatikvah" and cheers echoed throughout the hall.

Hirschl thought, "What a story this is!" He sprinted to his car, got in, and headed at breakneck speed to the office to submit it.

The joy of this day was short-lived for the next day the Arab armies attacked Israel.

Acknowledgments

I would like to thank the following individuals for their efforts on my work:

STUART KAHAN for being my mentor and friend throughout the process of creation of this novel and seeking a publisher for this book.

My Wilmington College faculty advisor for the Independent Study in Playwriting that started this journey was the late **DR. LEWIS R. MARCUSON** who read drafts of the play, "TRIUMPH ON THE GALLOWS", (the original title for my play) and provided detailed comment, support and encouragement.

My wife, **GAIL** for her continual love, support and encouragement shown to me.

My children **DEBORAH** and **STEVEN** for their ideas, support, love and encouragement for all my efforts.

My daughter-in-law **NICOLE,** who has always shared her love of family and has been such a loving helpmate to our son, Steven.

My brother **ALAN** and his wife, **MINDY** for their love and encouragement.

My publisher. **STEPHANIE LARKIN**, for welcoming me and my novel to Red Penguin Publishing and easing my way as a neophyte author.

My friends in Forest Hills, Bayside, or Douglaston who helped me to make theater come alive!

About the Author

Larry was born and raised in Queens, NY.

He graduated from Wilmington College of Ohio with a BA degree in Theater and then spent four decades working in Financial Services.

He was instrumental in founding and directing community theatre productions in Bayside and Forest Hills, New York.

Lawrence F. Bloom

His original musical for children, *Flip Flop*, is published by Dramasource.

He has written three original dramas for the stage: *We Look Forward*, *Dreamers Lullaby* and *Resistance*.

Fierce Resistance is his first novel, based upon his play.

Larry is married and lives with his wife and family in Queens, New York.